W9-DDK-425

ISLAND GIRL

Books by
Sandra Byrd
FROM BETHANY HOUSE PUBLISHERS

Girl Talk
Chatting With Girls Like You
A Growing-Up Guide
The Inside-Out Beauty Book
Stuff 2 Do

FRIENDS FOR A SEASON
Island Girl
Chopstick
Red Velvet

THE HIDDEN DIARY
Cross My Heart
Make a Wish
Just Between Friends
Take a Bow
Pass It On
Change of Heart
Take a Chance
One Plus One

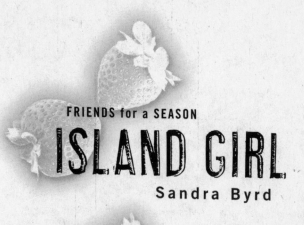

FRIENDS for a SEASON

ISLAND GIRL

Sandra Byrd

BETHANYHOUSE

MINNEAPOLIS, MINNESOTA

Island Girl
Copyright © 2005
Sandra Byrd

Cover design by Melinda Schumacher

Unless otherwise identified, Scripture quotations are from the HOLY BIBLE, NEW INTERNATIONAL VERSION®. Copyright © 1973, 1978, 1984 by International Bible Society. Used by permission of Zondervan Publishing House. All rights reserved.

Scripture quotations from Colossians are taken from the King James Version of the Bible.

Scripture quotations identified The Message are from *The Message*. Copyright © 1993, 1994, 1995 by Eugene H. Peterson. Used by permission of NavPress Publishing Group.

All rights reserved. No part of this publication may be reproduced, stored in a retrieval system, or transmitted in any form or by any means—electronic, mechanical, photocopying, recording, or otherwise—without the prior written permission of the publisher and copyright owners.

Published by Bethany House Publishers
11400 Hampshire Avenue South
Bloomington, Minnesota 55438

Bethany House Publishers is a division of
Baker Publishing Group, Grand Rapids, Michigan.

Printed in the United States of America

Library of Congress Cataloging-in-Publication Data

Byrd, Sandra.
    Island girl / by Sandra Byrd.
        p.   cm. — (Friends for a season)
      Summary: During her annual summer visit to the berry fields of her grandparents' farm on Sauvie Island, Oregon, thirteen-year-old Meg deepens her understanding of her unique characteristics and God's plan for her life.
    ISBN 0-7642-0020-8 (pbk.)
    [1. Grandparents—Fiction. 2. Islands—Fiction. 3. Friendship—Fiction. 4. Christian life—Fiction.] I. Title. II. Series: Byrd, Sandra. Friends for a season.
    PZ7.B9898Is   2005
    [Fic]—dc22   2005
                                          2004020635

For Samuel Byrd
My firstborn, only son,
and the best berry-picking pal
I have ever had

SANDRA BYRD lives near Seattle with her husband, two children, and a tiny Havanese circus dog named Brie. Besides writing *Island Girl* and the other FRIENDS FOR A SEASON books, Sandra is the best-selling author of the SECRET SISTERS SERIES, THE HIDDEN DIARY SERIES, and the nonfiction book collection GIRLS LIKE YOU.

Learn more about Sandra and her books at *www.friendsforaseason.com.*

PROLOGUE

I pulled my face away from the car window and wiped off the oily nose print with the cuff of my sweat jacket. I hoped I wouldn't break out in pimples within the hour. I already had a small one on the hairline by my forehead.

"Puberty," I muttered. Or stress. Thirteen was harder than I thought it would be. Maybe fourteen would be easier. I tried to catch a reflection of myself in the window to make sure everything else looked okay. Couldn't see the light freckles. Good. Hair tucked behind ear still, not greasy or puffed out. Good. Eyes looked gray in the window even though they were more water blue. I smiled at a funny billboard and caught a glimpse of my dimples. My only good feature, I thought, as far as my face was concerned. Maybe they'd make up for the zit.

"What did you say, Meg?" Mom never took her eyes from the road, keeping a steady speed. She wanted to get there before dark. She was nervous. I could tell.

"Nothing. Will they be waiting for us?"

"They always are."

I propped my legs on the dashboard. Even though it was twilight, I hoped for a little bit more sun. "Dashboard tan," my stepdad, Gary, called it.

I watched the car swallow the white divider lines in the road. My mom drives in the smooth middle lane, avoiding the ruts worn into the highway. She stays away from anything bumpy, even conversation. If I start to talk about something that's bothering me, Mom always brings us back into the safe middle again. I hate that.

The car gulped down a lump of uneven pavement. Even the center of the road isn't perfectly smooth.

"Will it work out okay?" I asked.

"It always does."

But it *doesn't* always work out okay.

I wanted to talk again about my choices. Would I go back to living with Mom and Gary and the new baby after the summer was over? Would I live with Grammy and Papa and Dad if Dad moved back to Oregon? Would they all be okay with whatever decision I made? Mom said she'd be fine with whatever I decided. She could certainly understand my wanting to spend some time getting to know my dad. I wondered if she really meant that.

I watched the telephone poles pacing the last few miles to the Island. Mom had said she wanted me to think over the decision on my own, and that was the end of the subject. So I didn't say anything about it, either, for now. I stuck to the smooth.

Mom turned the blinker on and we pulled off onto the gravel, crunching and grinding as we drove. You have to slow down when you drive on gravel or it gets thrown to the side of the road. That bugs the neighbors because gravel costs money. When you live in the country, you have to pay for the gravel yourselves.

"I guess you'll call me after the baby's born?"

Mom took her eyes off of the road for a second and winked. "I'll call you as soon as the baby is born, Meg. And we'll talk lots in between, of course."

She patted her tummy, and I did, too, probably for the last time. I mean, you don't go around patting your mom's stomach when she's not pregnant. It's weird enough as it is. Her stomach was round and hard as an orange in January under the faded T-shirt that said "Baby on Board." I thought it was totally embarrassing that she wore that. It's kind of goofy and old-fashioned. She said she wore it when she was pregnant with me, too. She seemed to hope those things would make the baby and me closer.

After a minute I felt the baby kick my hand and I smiled, but then I grew a little afraid. Would I like him or her? What if I didn't? If I wasn't really happy it would hurt everyone's feelings. They all wanted me to be happy. But I'm not a faker, and I just didn't know how I would feel. I kind of wanted a brother or a sister. But I kind of didn't.

I wondered if we'd be friends or if we even could be. I'll be a lot older than him or her. The baby would have its mom *and* its dad, my stepdad, Gary, living all together with us in Seattle.

My dad, on the other hand, was still in the army. He'd just written an email saying he'd be back on leave this summer—at Grammy and Papa's—and that he might be back to stay for good! Or he could go to Washington, D.C.

It might depend on me.

Mom turned the car and slowed down even more.

On Sauvie Island it's hard to see the houses from the gravel. Nobody lives right on the road; you have to turn off and drive in on the dirt a little, even to big houses. As we got closer, my stomach had its own hard lump. I zipped and then unzipped my sweat jacket. It made little metal rubbing noises. I tucked my hair behind my ears and then untucked one side. It looks better when you have one ear showing and one not showing.

A puff of dust announced our arrival. I saw the porch. There are always three rocking chairs there, like at the Three Bears' house. One for Papa Bear—that would be Papa—one for Mama Bear—that would be Grammy—and one for Baby Bear. That would be me.

The chairs have been there for so long that there are ruts worn into the porch boards. Grammy always says she dusts off the third chair each June, getting ready for my visit.

I warmed from the inside out. I wondered if she'd dusted it off already.

Papa stood up and waved. "Hey there, it's Meg!" he called. Grammy set aside a bucket of spring peas she was shucking. I love peas. A scientist named Mendel figured out how to grow peas so that they were all smooth, because most people like smooth peas better. That was the beginning of the study of genetics. Genetics is what you get from your mom and your dad, and it's what decides what you look like.

I like wrinkled peas best. I don't mind taking extra time to look for them at the farmers' market. I wondered if the baby inside my mom would look like me even though we have different dads.

I got out of the car and started walking to the porch. As soon as the dust cleared, I saw her. Someone was sitting in my chair! "Who is that?" I asked.

Mom shrugged. The girl sat right between my grandma and my grandpa, like she belonged to them. I zipped up my jacket and tugged my shorts into place. I tossed my backpack over my right shoulder and kept walking toward the porch.

When I got closer, our eyes locked. Hers were very dark, almost black. I knew right away this summer would be different in every way.

CHAPTER ONE

G rammy!" I ran up the stairs. Grammy wrapped me in her arms, soft like bread dough rising. I have a friend whose grandma runs marathons. I'm glad my Grammy's arms jiggle. Grammy smooched me on the forehead, then on each cheek.

"We've been waiting all day, Meg," she said. She ran her hands through my hair. "Still my strawberry blonde. You'll get blonder this summer. Your dad always did."

I patted her back.

The girl on the porch looked down. I stared at her, but she just kept looking down. Papa was already walking back up the steps with a suitcase. The second suitcase and my duffel bag sat on the ground next to the car. Mom started to pick up a bag, but Papa shook his head no. "Now, Nora, don't pick up that bag; it looks heavy." He gestured toward my mom's stomach and she smiled. "I'll bring this one up to Meg's room and be back down for the others." Papa had always made it easy for my mom to visit, even after the divorce.

Grammy turned to my mom and asked, "Can you stay the night? It's pretty late."

My mom shook her head. "No, I'll help Meg get settled and then I'm going back to finish my work in Portland. I've got to leave early in the morning and head back to Seattle."

Grammy gave her a sideways hug. I couldn't tell if Grammy was relieved or sorry that my mom was going home. She was always nice to Mom. I think it was easier when my mom wasn't there, though. It reminded Grammy of things she'd rather not think about and questions that she couldn't answer.

Grammy started into the house, then stopped and clapped her hands. "Where are my manners? Meg, this is Tia. Her family is staying on the farm this summer so her dad can run the farm for Papa. Since you're the same age, I thought it was a real blessing.

You'll have a friend to share everything with. Tia's family lives in a mobile home Papa bought for the back acreage."

Papa was getting old, but it wasn't like he'd had a heart attack or anything. Did he need that much help? Besides, what was *my* dad going to do if *her* dad ran the farm? A mobile home sounded permanent. Plus, she was still in my chair.

Tia looked up then. She didn't smile, but I sensed possibilities tucked behind the hard shell. I smiled and held out my hand. "My name is Meg. Nice to meet you." In spite of the questions I had, I guess that was honest. It's always nice to meet people. Even if I didn't know if they were coming or going.

She shook my hand. Her long black hair glistened with what little light was left of the fading day. "Nice to meet you, too." Her voice was soft American with little Spanish flecks, like scrambled eggs with a bit of salsa stirred in. She handed the bowl of peas she'd shucked to Grammy. "I'd better get home now. My mother will be waiting." Still no smile. So I didn't smile again. She hugged Grammy, who hugged her back tightly. Then Tia walked down the steps, around the house, and off to the back acreage. I wondered when I'd see her again.

Inside, the house was warm and bright, like always. It smelled like browned butter, greasy and rich, which meant cookies were waiting. Our house in Seattle wasn't very big, so it was awesome to come to Grammy and Papa's. I mean, they have a parlor, for heaven's sake. That's because the house is so old. Grammy's family was one of the first to settle on the Island, and she got to keep the house all these years. Papa was originally a city boy, but he was the better farmer now. He not only had a green thumb, he had black under his fingernails. Some on the Island were gentleman farmers, getting everyone else to do their work. Not Papa. I noticed, though, when he curled his fingers through his coffee mug handle, that his nails were a bit cleaner than I'd ever seen them in June. His hand shook a little, too. I hoped the coffee wouldn't burn him.

"Here, Nutmeg." That was Papa's nickname for me. At least Tia didn't have a nickname yet. Not one that I knew of, anyway.

I took one of the cookies off of the blue-and-white plate Papa held out. Chocolate chip. No nuts, no sprinkles, no dried fruit. I folded half a cookie into my mouth and wiped the sandy crumbs off of my lip. It had been a really hot day, which made baking cookies even more of a chore. My mom declined to take a cookie. I took a second one so Grammy wouldn't feel bad.

"I'd better get Meg unpacked a little, then get going. It's forty-five minutes back, and I'm getting tired," she said. She did have circles under her eyes. I'd wondered sometimes if she was too old to be having another baby, but I never said anything about it to Mom. It's not the kind of thing we could talk about even if we'd wanted to. I'd wanted to.

Papa hugged my mother. "I'm heading out to the barn, so I'll say my good-byes now," he said. "Be sure to let us know if there is anything we can do. We'll keep good care of Meggie, of course. And we'll let you know when Paul gets back."

Paul's my dad.

My mom nodded and hugged Papa. The stairway up to my room is one of those cool old-fashioned ones that coils like the licorice twists I eat all summer. Grammy keeps two kinds of twists for me, cherry and mixed berry, in a tall glass jar with a silver lid on it, like those jars they used to keep straws in. I never eat licorice unless I'm on Sauvie Island. Seriously. It's a special thing.

My mom and I wound our way up the stairs. "Papa was puffing as he brought your bags up," she whispered.

I nodded. "I'll be careful to not have him bring too much up here." Once we got into my room, I smiled. Goldilocks was *not* sleeping in my bed. It was all mine.

"Want me to help you unpack?" Mom asked. "I'd be glad to."

"Nah," I said. She'd want to organize my drawers all in a row or according to color or something, and I just like it my way. "Thanks for asking, though."

She smoothed the quilt on the bed and picked at

a loose piece of yarn tying the quilt squares together. "You going to be okay?"

"I always am," I said. Funny how the conversation had turned around.

"Yes. Well, have a good time. Not *too* good of a time, though." Mom laughed a little, but it didn't sound light. It was the closest she came to bringing up my choice to live with her or with Dad and her real feelings about it. I could see her switch gears as she kept smoothing wrinkles from the covers, and the conversation. "This certainly looks cozy. You'll sleep well."

I leaned over and hugged her. "We'll talk later this week, right?"

She nodded, and we went back down the stairs. After Mom had said good-bye to Grammy, Grammy handed her a bag of cookies. "For the road."

Mom smiled and thanked her. Then we walked out together to the car to say good-bye. I couldn't get close enough to hug her really tightly. Part of it was her tummy, but there are other things that keep people apart, too. She held my hand for almost a minute. Then she opened the car door, got in, and started the engine. Before backing away from the car, I impulsively knocked on the window three times. I-Love-You.

She looked at me and knocked back, four times. I-Love-You-Too. She had tears in her eyes. I did, too.

Later that night I unpacked my things. Waiting in

the top drawer was the latest teen devotional.

Grammy. Really. Grammy always wanted me to know what God thought about this or that, which was really sweet in some ways. I was interested in what He thought, too, but I kind of wanted to find out what God says on my own without Grammy's help. I had to admit, I hadn't had much success yet. Maybe I didn't speak the language.

I turned the light out and stared out the window. My breath formed a spot of steam, and I drew a smiley face in it. I reached under the windowsill. Ha! I felt the hard little nubs against my fingertips. My gum collection was still there. Grammy hadn't found it yet. It's very cool that gum doesn't mold.

In the distance, on the back acreage, I saw flickering lights. Tia's new house. I could see a lot in the dark. I slipped into bed.

One year when I was a little girl, some friends of Grammy and Papa's came to stay for a week during the summer. They were from the East Coast, and they had a girl my age. I think I was about seven, maybe eight. I can't remember. Anyway, that girl was a total pill. Everyone thought we were going to be best pals because we were the same age. I felt like saying, I've got a class full of twenty-five kids at school and I'm only friends with like six or seven of them. Just being the same age doesn't mean you're going to be friends. Anyway, we finally found one thing we both liked doing—dress up. In the attic Grammy kept a bunch of old clothes and jewelry from way back. Since things were warming up, I decided to show this girl. She liked it okay, but when she went back East she took at least half of Grammy's jewelry with her. What was I going to say? If I didn't share, I'd be selfish, and I knew that really, Grammy had been generous to share it all with me. The worst part was, I'd planned to give her a piece or two—whichever ones she wanted. No holdbacks. I was glad that girl never visited again.

CHAPTER TWO

The next few days Papa and Grammy and I mainly hung around the house getting reacquainted. I guess Tia was giving us some space, because I hadn't seen her at all since that first night.

Toward the end of my first week back I was running down the road. Not running away, you know, running for sport. I was on the track team and had to keep in shape for fall. Pretty soon my legs had gray gravel dust

23

coating them from the knees down. That was definitely not helping my dashboard tan. I wasn't sure which had more grit inside—my shoes or my mouth. When the thought came to me that they both had tongues, I figured I had runner's high and had better quit for the day.

On either side of the driveway were acres and acres of fields. Raspberry, blueberry, and strawberry fields. I stood stock-still in the middle of the driveway, letting the sun bake the skin on my arms. It's weird—when your skin is really hot or really cold the goose bumps come out. They lumped between the hairs on my arms. I hated that hair. I had way too much of it on my arms, and, of course, you can't very well shave your arms like you can your legs.

I kept my eyes closed. The strawberries were red, perfectly ripe. Their perfume swirled all around me. Every summer of my whole life I had been in those fields. Picking fruit, keeping Papa company. Digging dirt with him. Tasting berries and offering my opinion. Kid noises brought me back to the present— squawking and squealing and giggling. My eyes opened and I looked to the back acreage. Tia's house.

Maybe I'd go and visit. Maybe. Later.

"Hi there, Meg m'dear." Mrs. Jenkins stopped me at the end of the road to our property. Her fingernails looked like the ones you used to see on old Chinese men—you know, the pond water–colored nails that curled around because they were so long. Kind of like dreadlocks. Let them grow, don't wash too often, see what happens. Dreadlocks are cool. Grimy nails are not. She handed the mail to me. "How is summer going?"

"Great," I answered. And it was. I was a little bored, but not too bad yet.

"I'm glad you're back," Mrs. Jenkins said. "Your grandparents get lonely, I think. Lots of friends, little family." She nodded, and her big bouffant hairdo shook like a teakettle as she drove off in the mail jalopy. In some strange way even Mrs. Jenkins felt like family to me. After all, she'd probably been growing those same fingernails since I was born.

I walked up the driveway, riffling through the mail. I saw a letter from Germany. My heart thumped twice fast. Dad! Me, he emailed, or we called. Grammy and Papa didn't want to figure out how to do email and had no computer, so Dad wrote actual letters to them, but not very often. This must be something important. I overcame the temptation to open the letter, read it, and pretend it had been mangled in the mail. I'd know what he said in a few minutes. Grammy wouldn't wait long to read it.

"Grammy! The mail is here." I walked into the house.

Grammy pottered into the hallway.

"There's a letter from Dad," I said, flicking it to the top of the stack. She opened it right there. That was a great thing about Grammy. She wasn't one of those kinds of people who wanted to walk off and read it in private.

"He's coming!" She flapped the page at me like a dove wing. "He'll be home next month. Maybe for several weeks. And," she kept reading, "he reminds us, 'Maybe for much longer.'" She read a section out loud: "'I am up for promotion and a move to Washington, D.C.—or retirement and back to Sauvie Island. Either one would bring big changes for all of us, and we can talk about that more when I get there. I'm looking forward to settling into a real home. Will see you then.'"

He was coming home, and soon. And maybe for good! I pulled out from under my T-shirt a cameo necklace. You know, the kind with a blue background and a girl's profile in ivory on top. "Do you remember when Daddy gave this to me?" Grammy nodded. "Well, I keep it on all the time. It makes me feel close to him, even when he's far away, you know?"

Grammy giggled and pulled a black cameo necklace out from under her shirt. "He must have been on a necklace-buying kick that year," she said. "Or else he ran out of other ideas." Grammy liked to keep things around that reminded her of Dad. I did, too. For example, I knew the blue-and-white plates Grammy used for cookies were from Holland, which is really close to Germany. My dad bought those for Grammy every Christmas. My mom even had one or two still that my dad had given her before the divorce. We lived here while Dad lived in Germany, and that had been part of the whole problem. Mom didn't use her plates anymore.

I whirled Grammy around the kitchen and then wiped the sweat from my brow. "It's great!" I could see her mind working. She was planning to get his room ready. I knew Grammy. I knew my dad. I loved them both.

I headed upstairs to shower and then change. I pitched my clothes on the floor, but then I picked them up and lobbed them into the hamper. My mom really cares that Grammy doesn't have to pick up after me. Maybe she's worried that Grammy and Papa were judging how Mom raised the only child of their only child. Maybe they *were* judging, I don't know, but it wasn't my problem. When I looked out my window, I saw Tia out on the property. She was running around with a little boy, playing tag. I couldn't see too much from this distance, but watching them, I got an idea. I felt so good, and I wanted to share my happiness.

I ran downstairs and tracked Grammy down in the barn, where Papa was tinkering with some strawberry plants. Again.

"Can I bake some cookies?" I asked.

"Now? There are a couple left over from the other day," she answered.

"No, I want to try." My cooking skills were not, shall we say, world famous.

"Okay. But remember, it's hot out. It's going to be hotter in the kitchen."

"That's okay. They're for something special."

I headed into the kitchen. It *was* hot. Really hot. I turned the oven on anyway.

You know, I never was the kind of girl to do things straight up. I got a bag of white chips out and mixed them in with the milk chocolate chips in the batter. Then I threw in some dried cranberries.

I remembered this one day when I was watching the Food Network. I've always watched more than I've baked. Someone had made cranberry cookies. Everyone in the audience loved them. I wanted these cookies to be really great. Impressive, actually.

Finally they smelled done. I pulled them out of the oven. "Grammy?" She was still in the barn. I tried to figure out what to do next. Should I get them off of the hot pan? I slid the spatula under the first cookie. Then the next. They wrinkled. By the time I got to the second sheet the cookies had cooled some and they slipped right off. The house smelled like browned butter, and the cookies looked great. I put them on a plate—a blue-and-white plate. I was set. I went upstairs to put on my swimsuit and then left for the beach, which sounded really good about now.

"Hey," I called to Papa in the barn, "I'm heading for Reeder Beach." Grammy was out inspecting the raspberry vines, which were just beginning to flower.

Papa waved me over. "Look, Nutmeg! I'm almost

there. This will be the inheritance that makes you rich!" he said. Papa was always tinkering with equipment and plants.

I walked over to get a look. Papa smelled like aftershave. For the longest time I couldn't figure out why he always smelled more like aftershave than other guys. Then I'd seen him slap some on his bald head one morning. More territory to cover.

I leaned over the mound. "What is it?"

He put his arm around me. "It's a strawberry." I tried to keep some excitement in my face, but it looked kind of like every other berry mound on either side of the house all the way toward the Richards' property.

"Not just any berry. A super berry," he said. "I'm crossing one berry with another to come up with a completely new breed. I've got a little under an acre of them planted, experimenting. The University of Oregon is interested. They'll be out here in a week, at the height of my season, to check it out. If they like it, they might sell them all over the country." I had to admit, the berries looked good. They smelled great, too.

Papa handed a berry to me and I bit into it. *Divine*.

"All those years of my asking you to taste and weed and feed and pull are going to pay off, Meggie girl," Papa said. "Hey, you got the juice all over your lip. Better wipe it off. It looks like lipstick," he said.

I grinned, grabbed my bike, and rode off. Lipstick, eh? Maybe I'd leave it on. Never knew who I'd run into. I was on my way to Reeder Beach, of course. But first I rode to the back acreage.

The mobile house looked very, very nice. In the backyard a line full of clothes flapped in the wind. The bleach scent of the sheets mingled with the candy smell of the berries and the wormy sniff of dirt. That's what summer should smell like. I saw Tia's mom first. "Hello," I said. "Is Tia here?"

The mom looked at me and shook her head. "No Tia," she said. "Later."

Okay, I could come back later.

I caught a glimpse of a little guy in soccer shorts and well-worn cleats, with a big gap in his smile. I kicked the soccer ball toward him as I got on my bike, and he tossed it up in the air and bonked it with his head. I smiled at him and biked off. I wondered how long "later" meant. Not that it really mattered.

The road to Reeder Beach is really long. There are marshes on either side. Sauvie Island isn't very far from Portland, so a lot of city people come there in the summer. Most of them pick berries or buy already-picked flats. Some of them find our beach on the Columbia River, so they come to hang out. That means there is a lot of traffic. Whether you're running or biking, you have to make sure the city people don't run you off the road.

I pulled my bike into the driveway of the Minit Mart on the bluff before the beach. Old Mark was at the Minit Mart, alone. He had been running the store from forever. Okay, he wasn't old, but he was married, so that was old enough, and maybe he hadn't been running it forever, but he had ever since I could remember. "What's up?" he asked.

"Not much." I bought a Coke and headed to the beach. I liked it that he didn't ask me how I was or how my year was or anything like that. He just treated me like I was here all the time. Like I belonged.

The beach felt good on my toes, and I lay on the sand for a while, tossing my T-shirt to the side so I could tan in my suit. There were lots of people there—Portlanders, mostly, but some Islanders, too. No kids, really. Just older people. No girls. I don't know why, but there weren't very many girls on the Island. Not my age, anyway. I think it was because so many farms had sold out. After a couple of hours I decided to check back and see about Tia. I tossed on my T-shirt and went back into the Minit Mart.

"Hey, Mark. Do you have any new movies to rent?" He waved toward the DVD section in the back, kind of by the milk. Something was leaking in that store. The milk area always smelled a little off, like a dirty dishrag.

Carefully, I looked through each movie. There were some Spanish selections, but Tia wouldn't need those. Her English seemed fine. I finally chose an old one that I had already seen about a mother and a daughter who trade places. I might be a little bored, but at least I knew it was good. I paid Mark, tucked the movie into my little backpack, and pedaled off.

As soon as I pulled onto the property, I saw Tia's mom out front with the little boy. Tia's dad was fiddling with a tractor. That tractor was older than I was. It was helpful that he knew how to keep it running.

I held out my hand. "Hello, I'm Meg." Her mother nodded.

She seemed to already know who I was. "Ava Ramos," she said, pointing to herself. She tousled the little boy's hair. "Pablo."

I wished I had introduced myself last time. I didn't know why I hadn't.

"Is Tia here?" I asked. Why was my voice shaky?

"Un momento," Mrs. Ramos said. She disappeared inside the house.

"Psst, hey, Pablo." He looked at me. "Do you like licorice?" I handed him a cherry twist. He grinned and peeled a string off and then slid it back and forth through the gap in his teeth, like dental floss.

"Gracias," he said, then ran off toward his dad. Tia came out of the house.

"Hello," she said. She smiled shyly this time.

"Um, hi." Voice still shaky. No more Cokes for me. "I wondered if you'd like to come over and watch a movie tonight. After dinner. And have some cook-ies."

She looked at her mother, who nodded toward Tia's father. Tia walked over and talked with him. He stopped tinkering long enough to pull her close for a few words, then went back to the machinery.

Tia slowly walked back toward me. "No, thank you." I couldn't read her expression. Sad? Angry? Joyous? More like blank. We both just stood there for a minute. Pablo was trying to get into my backpack, and his mother scolded him into the house. Since there was nothing else to say, I just said, "Okay. Good-bye." Then I hopped on my bike and rode back to the barn.

No, thank you. Just like that. Not "How about another time," or "I'm busy tonight," or "Thanks for inviting me." At least no one could blame me for not trying. I stubbed my toe on a rock on the way to the barn, and tears sprang to my eyes. Both eyes, and it hadn't even hurt that much. I stood my bike against the wall and headed toward the house.

When I got close enough I saw someone standing in the doorway talking to Grammy. A very tall some-one. A very boy someone. I brushed my hands across my face and blinked fast ten times to clear my eyes.

"Meg! Charlie's here returning a saw. I just offered him one of your cookies."

Charlie Richards? He used to be way shorter than I was. Really scrawny legs. Now he was at least half a foot taller than I. Not scrawny at all.

"Hi, Meg," he said. "Good cookies. A little doughy, though."

"Thanks." I screwed up my face.

"I noticed you biking in. Decide to leave running to the boys?"

My eyes narrowed. "Some of us are able to do both," I said. Apparently not all of him had changed.

He stuck his hands into his pockets and pulled on his cap. "I'm just joking. The Island team is running the Hood to Coast this year. Actually, the teens run from Portland to the coast since it's about the halfway mark—not as long as all the way from Mount Hood. I wondered if you'd be interested in joining the team as an alternate. You're thirteen, right?"

"Yes." Charlie was fourteen, I thought. I couldn't remember. It hadn't seemed really important before, but it did now. I think he was one year older than I. Sometimes I didn't really feel like a teen, more like a kid still. Sometimes more like a woman. It was confusing.

"Meg?"

Oh yeah. I refocused on Charlie. "Yeah."

"If you're interested, I'll get the details from our coach, Kiski. I didn't want to ask him till I saw if you were here and interested. He's got the final say on if you're on the team or not."

"I'm interested," I said. I love running. Besides, what else did I have to do?

"Great." Charlie snagged another cookie from the blue-and-white plate. "I'll come by later this week and let you know if you're on. Okay? We run in August. We train till then." He turned the cookie over. "Hope these underbaked cookies don't make me sick." He winked at me and turned pink. I think I was a little more grown-up than he'd expected, too, and he broke a joke to play for time. He gave a little half wave and ran off.

After dinner I asked Grammy and Papa if they wanted to watch the movie with me. I wasn't surprised when they politely declined, because they'd already been yawning. I explained about how I had got it to watch with Tia, but how she wasn't interested in being friends. "We'll watch it with you, then," Grammy said. "We might like it!"

I wasn't up for charity right then. "Nah. I've already seen it. I guess I'll go get the bird feeders out."

"Wonderful! Been waiting for you to do that," Papa said. His scalp turned red. It always did that when he tried too hard.

I staked the bird feeders out every year when I came. I always hung the hummingbird ones on the porch, which wrapped all the way around Grammy and Papa's house. That way Grammy could see them no matter what room she was in. We didn't put too many other bird feeders out, though. The birds tend to eat the berries, so some people think they're pests and don't want them around. I don't think they're pests. Bluebirds, especially, are so pretty, so small. Sometimes I wonder if they ever get tired of flying from one home to the next, winter in one place, summer in another. I wonder if they'd just as soon stay in Oregon for a while and see what it was like to stay put in a place that had always been home.

CHAPTER THREE

I t isn't often that I get anonymous presents. Seriously. Before that Sunday morning I don't think I had ever gotten a secret gift, and *this* one was left on the doorstep. Right then and there I wished I had someone to share the news with, to wonder who it was from. Somebody my age, a friend. I could call someone at home later, I supposed, but it wouldn't have been the same. I got a surprise in church, too. So it was a totally unusual day.

The morning had started out normally. First we went to church, and that was okay. I sat between Grammy and Papa, trying not to be overcome by waves of rose perfume and spice aftershave. It was almost two weeks into June and getting hot earlier in the day. The music was really slow, and I was kind of tired because I'd been up late reading, so I kept pinching the soft skin on the inside of my arm, trying to stay awake. I went to church in Seattle, but we had a youth group, and that was more fun. I was with other kids my own age. We had loud music and a crazy leader, Jack, who everyone loved. Here it was kind of . . . old. My family had been going here since Noah's Ark bumped up on dry ground. But maybe the quiet was good. I was singing a hymn, and all of a sudden I felt God talking directly to me. It surprised me to know so clearly that it was Him. The words went like this:

> Softly and tenderly Jesus is calling,
> Calling for you and for me;
> See, on the portals He's waiting and watching,
> Watching for you and for me.
> Come home, come home,
> You who are weary, come home;
> Earnestly, tenderly, Jesus is calling,
> Calling, O sinner, come home!

I had no idea what portals are, but from head to toe I felt peaceful, like someone had taken His hand and smoothed the wrinkles out of me like Mom had with my quilt. *I want to be home, Jesus. But where is home for me?*

Then when we got home, there it was. The anonymous gift. Propped up against the door. A bundle of flowers held together with a pretty knit string tie. The flowers were mostly the kinds of wild flowers you could find anywhere on the Island right now. The fields were aflame with yellow and blue and pink heads flickering with even the least sigh of the wind.

Papa picked it up. "Do you have a secret admirer?" he asked Grammy.

Grammy twinkled. She pointed to a square of paper with a letter *M* sticker on it, tied on. "As far as I know, Meg is the only *M* in the house. Must be for her."

I took the flowers and stuck my nose deep in the heart of them. They didn't really smell like anything. That was okay. It'd be hard to compete for smell on an island covered with growing berries. The flowers sure looked pretty, though, especially with that knitted string tie. I opened my mouth, and just as I was about to ask how old Charlie Richards was, I caught myself. I didn't need to know that badly. Not right now. But *could* it have been him? I was pretty jazzed.

Papa went to take a nap. Grammy padded into the kitchen.

"I'm hungry," I said. "What's for lunch?"

"Leftover meatloaf sandwiches. But don't eat too much. We're having company for dinner."

"Really?" I grabbed some squishy white bread—the kind I never get to eat at home, the kind that sticks to the roof of your mouth—and slathered mayo on it. "Who's coming?" I took cold meatloaf out of the fridge and settled a slab on my bread. Grammy baked meatloaf with bacon tied around it. It was so good.

"Tia."

I counted till ten before answering. Actually, after I counted till ten I took a bite and swallowed it and counted to ten again. I thought that showed a lot of restraint. "Really. Why?"

"I thought you might enjoy it."

"I might. Maybe. But I bet she won't come. She didn't want to come over last week."

"Papa talked with her father about that. He said he told Tia no because he didn't want to overstep and offend. He was being careful because he works for us; we're his employers as well as his neighbors. We don't invite them to many things because we try to be careful and respectful of their way of life, too. Not only that, they may not want to be with us on their off hours since they're often with us all day."

I nodded. It seemed really sad, though. "I see. I want to be respectful, but I want to include people, too. Learn more about them and have them learn about me. However do you get close to people otherwise?"

Grammy nodded. "Building new lives and keeping hold of what's important from the past is not easy to balance, and it's harder for those who are new, like the Ramoses, and for those who are old, like the old-time Islanders. Papa wanted to make sure he didn't make anything uncomfortable for them, and they look out for that with us, too. Now, why don't you go clean your room? You don't want Tia to see it a mess."

She could switch topics with the best of them, my grandmother. I hauled myself up the stairs. The room was clean! But I knew Grammy would play detective with me anyway. Are the clothes put in the right drawers? Is anything under your bed? I could have told you right then that if Tia was going to come in and check under my bed and make sure my dresser drawers were organized there was no hope we'd be friends. It didn't matter *whose* culture approved or disapproved.

I poked my head under the bed out of respect for my grandmother. Three dust bunnies cowered in the corner, out of my reach. I made a halfhearted attempt to swipe at them. Instead, my hand bonked against something sharp. I reached in, practically dislocating my shoulder in the process.

I pulled out a gold frame with a picture inside it. It was the most beautiful picture of a raspberry field. Row upon row of raspberry canes strung along barbed wire. Raspberry canes look kind of like candy canes—they are shaped like them, tall with a curling head, like an upside down J or a shepherd's staff. The berries grow all up and down them. On top it said, *John 15:1–13,* with all thirteen verses printed out. In the corner of the picture was written a date and *To Paul, in thanks for good service. Future Farmers of America, Sauvie Island.* My heart skipped. My dad had actually held this when he was a boy. I didn't have many things that had been my dad's. What were his dreams? Were Grammy and Papa thinking he would be a farmer—and were they mad when he went into the army instead? I'd have to ask him when he got here.

I crawled up onto the bed and rested, drifting into a long summer's nap. I awoke to a knock at the front door. Oh no! Tia was here! I leaped out of bed, ran my hands across the top of it, and flipped the pillow. I pulled my hair back into little star clips. I'd kind of resisted wearing them before—too girly girl. They looked pretty, though, I had to admit. I looked older.

I met Tia at the door. Ha! Many years of racing to get ready before the bus came had paid off. "Hi," I said.

"Hi." This time she smiled full on and her eyes shone. Maybe there was hope. I mean, it wasn't her fault if her dad had told her she couldn't come over last time, right?

We went into the kitchen and I saw her look at my little flower bouquet, which Grammy had put in the center of the table. I almost told Tia how I got it, but we weren't at that level, you know? Sometimes when you try to rush a friendship it ends up back-firing and you feel too goopy right up front and then it all goes bad.

"Come on to the meal," Grammy called out.

"Thank you for inviting me," Tia said as we sat at the table. Her nails were nice. I liked that. I don't like it when girls rush around with fake nails falling off, or six long nails and four that broke off but they can't bring themselves to cut the last six down.

Grammy served the pasta salad. For once Papa didn't burp. He always says it's important that some-one in the family act like a man. I hoped he could keep his manly "manners" away for a couple more hours.

"How long have you been here?" I tried to open with something nice to start the conversation.

"A few weeks. My father brought us up from Mexico when Papa offered him the new house." She called him "Papa," not "your Papa." She went on. "Our school session was over, anyway. Some sum-mers my mom and Pablo and I get to come up and stay with my dad. Some years we don't. This year seemed like a good year to come back since we have our own house." Her eyes sparkled when she said that—"our own house."

I told her all about everyone on the Island. I told her about my school in Seattle. I told her about the tree house by Reeder Beach that my dad and I had built way back in the marshland. No one else knew where to find it, only my dad and me.

She told me about her home in Mexico. We talked music. We talked hobbies and likes and dislikes. We chatted without having to stop and think of things to talk about. I liked her a lot.

After dinner Grammy led us into the parlor. "I have an idea for you girls," she said.

Uh-oh.

"Do you know the old shack?"

I did. It was on the edge of the property, kind of where our land meets the Richardses', near the road.

"It's in poor shape, I know," Grammy went on. "It needs some boards to be tightened up, and a little paint. When I was a girl, we sold berries there."

"That was quite some time ago," Papa joked. Grammy didn't laugh. "Paul tried to do a berry stand there, too, if I remember rightly. It didn't work out for him. Too much competition even then," Papa continued. Grammy still stared at him. She wasn't smiling, and he picked up the vibe. "I think I'll wander out to the barn," he said, and then he left.

"Anyway, when I was a girl we'd pick berries and sell them to Portlanders. You know, like many of the other farms on the Island do right now. We made gobs of money. Gobs for us girls, anyway. It's a little place, but it's got a nice signage and room for the two of you to sit and a cash register and a stack of boxes."

Grammy settled into her chair and looked thoughtful. "I thought perhaps you'd like to take a day or two, paint it up, and then sell some berries. You can pick whatever you like from the fields, alongside the workers. When it's raspberry season you'll have to take the fruit deep inside the vines that the machines can't get to, but they'd still be free. The money would be yours to keep. I just know you girls can make it happen. Ozzie has told me that you're quite a businesswoman." She winked at Tia. "And I know Meg always has something clever up her sleeve. Won't your dad be surprised to come home and find you running the shack successfully?"

I looked at Tia, who didn't look either positive or negative but was looking at Grammy, who beamed. Grammy wanted us to do this. We both knew it. "I guess we could," I said. "If you want to." It would be fun to have something successful to show Dad.

Tia said, "I do." She looked at Grammy for approval. Grammy gave it to us both.

"You'll have to get to work soon because the other operations on the Island are already selling berries," Grammy said. "There's paint in the barn, and some nails and hammers. You'll have to be there most of the day. Picking in the morning, packing, then selling."

"I don't have much else to do," I said to Tia. "Do you?"

She shook her head. "My father—"

"I already spoke with him," Grammy said. "He said it's fine. He can keep an eye on you while you're in the fields and he's supervising the other workers." She turned toward the barn. "Don't let Papa help, though. He's not as young as he thinks he is." Worry wrinkled across Grammy's forehead. Papa was seventy-five. I remembered, since I put three quarters in his birthday card last year. It wasn't easy getting older.

"Don't worry, we can do it on our own. Or else we'll ask Tia's dad for help. Okay! Let's go look at the shack before it gets too dark!" I slipped on my flip-flops and Tia did, too, and we ran across the field.

She wasn't a runner. I could tell by the way she kind of jogged along, more like a dancer—flowery, but not fast. Her hair trailed along behind her like a veil. Maybe I should grow my hair long again.

"This is it?" She stopped at the shack. Since she'd been living here for a month or so already, she knew where it was.

"This is it! Wait!"

I raced back to the barn and got a couple of padded chairs, the ones Grammy used when her old lady friends came for game night.

It was already twilight outside, but we could see what needed to be done.

"I think if your dad will help us get all of the boards tight, we can do the painting. We have some stepladders."

"My dad will help. He'll be proud of me—part owner in an American business! Earning money!" Tia grinned. "What color do you think we should paint it?" she asked.

"Well, we have red and white paint, mostly, because those are the barn colors. I don't think we should do white. I mean, everyone whitewashes. But if we do red, then people will think it's just a barn."

"How about mixing them? How about pink?" she suggested.

Pink. I never thought of pink. "It would be different," I admitted. "It would set us apart. Plus, as two girls, we could kind of make a theme out of that, you know? Good idea."

She softened and smiled. I got the idea she hadn't heard "good idea" too often.

"Do you mind collecting the money, you know, when we sell the berries?" Tia asked. "I kind of feel funny about it."

I didn't know why she felt funny, but that was okay. Maybe she hated math. I could understand that. I, myself, preferred to read. "I'll do the money. No problem."

"Thanks."

Someone was walking toward the shack, but I couldn't tell who it was since the light was behind him. "Hi!" he called out. Charlie! I rubbed my neck a little to activate any Love's Baby Soft left over from that morning and ran my fingers through my hair.

"Hi," I said back.

He nodded politely at Tia and then turned toward me. "I came to tell you—Kiski says you're in."

All of a sudden it came rushing back to me. The Portland to Coast team. "What would it involve again?"

Charlie looked puzzled. "You know, training with the team a couple of hours every day. The hours change because we go when Kiski is free from work. Then running with us—to win—at the end of the season. No bellyaching. No rule bending."

I looked at Charlie. His eyes looked even bluer in this light. Water blue, baby blue. Never noticed that before. I *couldn't* be free any time during the day. Tia didn't want to handle the money. Even if she did, she couldn't pick berries alone or run the place alone for a couple of hours each day. We couldn't have the stand some days and not others. Then I looked at Tia. She was pretty even when she was looking at the ground. I realized that they probably didn't know each other. I have to admit, I wasn't altogether in a hurry to introduce them, but I did it anyway.

"Charlie, this is my friend Tia. Tia, this is Charlie. He lives next door."

Charlie stuck his hand out and shook hers. She shook his hand and her beautiful black hair swept around her. "Pleased to meet you."

I, however, was still thinking about the team. My legs ached to do that run. Wouldn't *that* be something to show my dad when he came back? He was a runner, too. But Tia wasn't. And I had already promised to do the berry stand, although I wished I hadn't. I didn't want to run the booth and be Miss Sacrificial. I wanted to be on the Portland to Coast team—still be Tia's friend, you know, but not give that all up. I wished I had remembered about the run before I'd said anything.

But I hadn't. I cleared my throat and swallowed my sadness. "I won't be able to be on the team after all. Tia and I are going to run a berry stand."

Charlie's eyes opened wide, and he took his baseball cap off and scratched his head. "What? Where?"

"Right here." My arm swept toward the shack. "We're going to paint it. Pink."

"Pink? Man, you know you're never going to make any money. We are way out on the end of the road. Hardly anyone ever drives down here, except people who live here. And they already have all the berries they want. My brother and I tried a stand years ago. We ended up with a lot of moldy berries."

I hadn't thought about that end-of-the-road thing. Maybe that's why my dad hadn't made any money way back when. "We'll make plenty of money." I tried to sound more certain than I felt.

"Yeah, yeah. Oh well. You're passing up a good opportunity to get a slot on the team. Who knows if there will be one next time? I'll be here when you sign the bankrupt papers on the 'Pink Palace.'"

I frowned. "It's past your bedtime, I think. Better get home."

He smiled. "I should get going. Let me know if you change your mind before tomorrow's practice. It's nice to meet you, Tia. I'm sure I'll see you around."

Tia smiled. "You too."

Charlie jogged off. I just sat there. I really did want to be on the team. I'd seen them run before, but this was the first year I was old enough to run on it myself. Running is the one thing I am good at, the only place I ever shine. I supposed the berry stand might work out. But it also might all be over in a week or two and then I would have given away the chance to run—for nothing.

"Are you sure you want to do this?" I asked. I wanted to get to know her, suddenly, as a potential friend. But I didn't want to butt in on her world, like Grammy had worried about. I was an old-timer Islander, although I wasn't old. Tia was a new Islander, but she seemed open and brave.

She nodded, eyes shining. "Oh yes."

Tia needed to get home; it was dark. The frogs were out again, courting. On my way back to the house, I passed Papa in the barn, bending over his plants. He looked old. I had the sudden impulse to run into the barn and hug him, so I did. The scent of his Old Spice aftershave hugged the space around me. Papa waved me off, but I saw the grin.

Grammy was rearranging some pictures in the room that she was getting ready for Dad. "If it's longer than a visit," she said cheerfully, "he'll need his own house. I don't think he'll want the guest room forever." I snuck away without saying anything and stopped in the kitchen to get a glass of water. I saw my secret bouquet with the nicely knitted string and softened toward Charlie.

"Do you have any yarn?" I asked Grammy as she came into the room.

"Oh yes. Going to knit? Wondered if you'd dropped that habit."

"Ha ha." That was our joke. Dropping knitting, like I'd dropped a stitch.

"Yes, I have a few skeins of light blue cashmere that I had every intention of using up before the gears in my hands got stuck." I looked at her fingers. Early arthritis had gnarled and knobbed them like an old tree.

I sat in bed later, cuddling the baby blue yarn. Actually, water blue, the color of blue eyes. What to knit? Getting an anonymous knitted present had made me feel like knitting a gift for someone else.

What, though, I didn't know. I just started knitting a
row. I could decide later.

*When I got to seventh grade, I could finally run
track. I had always run as a little girl, but just around
the block or as part of the soccer team.*

*Finally I was on a team. A team where everyone
worked together and looked out for one another and
cheered one another on. A place to belong. A place to be
valued. Somewhere to fit where I didn't feel like the odd
man out. That's what I ran for. That's kind of what I live
for. To stay on the team.*

CHAPTER FOUR

Two days later we had the shack almost done. Really. I hadn't worked so hard since Gary and my mom decided to remodel the kitchen. It was already the middle of June, edging a little toward July. Prime berry time. We had to keep moving.

Tia had her hair twisted back so it wouldn't get pink with paint. It reminded me of my candy stash, so I offered her a licorice twist. She took it and unwrapped the strands one by one. That's how I ate mine, too. "So, what do you think you're going to spend your money on?" she asked me.

"Money?"

"You know, that we make from the booth this summer. We've got like nine or ten weeks left to make some money. Grammy said she made gobs of money." There it was again. Grammy. Not "your Grammy." I tried to let it go.

"I don't know. Running stuff, I guess. I need some more shoes. The good ones are like a hundred dollars a pair, and I'm going to need two pairs next year. Some warm-up suits. Sports fees. Uniform fees. There's not going to be a lot of money at my house now because, well . . ." I had to decide. Do I tell her? I do.

"My mom is going to have a baby. In August. So that costs a lot of money, and she didn't save hardly anything from when I was a baby, so there is a lot of baby gear to buy."

Tia sat on the padded chair, swinging her legs. "Very nice! Is your dad happy about the baby?"

I sucked in my breath. "I guess so. I don't know. My mom and dad have been divorced for a long time and my mom is remarried. My stepdad's name is Gary."

"Do you like him?" She clapped her hand over her mouth. "I'm sorry. Too personal."

"No, it's okay. I do like him. He's very sweet. He always buys me books, and he's the only one who can pick out books I like besides me."

Tia kept swinging her feet. "I never thought about you not having enough money for anything you wanted. I mean"—she pointed toward the house and the barn—"you seem to have everything you want."

"I do have more here," I admitted. I dipped up the brush and kept painting. That was kind of a new thought. Maybe it would be financially easier on everyone if I wasn't living in Seattle. Maybe it would be a relief to my mom and to Gary, instead of having to buy everything for me. Sometimes, when I thought about Mom and Gary and the new baby, I kind of wondered if I would still be connected to everyone or sticking out as different in some way.

"Let's finish the last part and go swimming," I said. "Have you been to Reeder Beach yet?"

Tia shook her head. "I haven't been to very many places. I go to St. John's a lot with my mom to visit my aunts and cousins. They mostly live over there. Before this year, whenever I've been here in the summer, we've all stayed together in St. John's." St. John's was over the bridge a few miles away. I hadn't been there for a long time.

Tia dipped her brush and did the trim. Slowly, to make sure it was all covered. I noticed how careful she was. I was kind of, like, artistic and free flowing. She was very precise.

"What are you going to spend your money on?" I asked her. "The gobs and gobs of money." We both broke out in giggles.

"I don't know. Maybe some new clothes. I'm hoping to go to school here." She didn't seem to want to say much. I thought I should wait for her even though I usually fill in the gaps of silence.

"I hope that we can stay here all year now. So that my family can live together. Plus, the schools are very good here. My dad was sending extra money back to Mexico so I could go to a good school. Here, good schools are free."

"Is that where you learned to speak such good English, at your school?" I asked.

"Yes. And other things. But in order to do that we had to live with my grandmother. I think my mother wanted her own home." She looked off toward where her mother was arranging some potted geraniums on the porch of the house on the back acreage. "She's very happy. My dad is happy here, and Pablo starts school this year."

I guess I hadn't really thought too long and hard about them living here forever. I mean, all year. Even when I wasn't here. Had everyone talked about that already? Had a decision been made?

"My dad enjoys helping Papa," she said. "He's good on a farm, and he cares about Papa."

"I see that," I said. "Your dad is a great farmer." Her dad really was very good on the farm. But *my* dad cared about Papa the most. My dad could learn to farm. He could stay here and help. He could do anything, if he wanted to stay.

We finished up painting and stood back. "Whaddya think?" I asked.

"I think it looks great." She came close to me and rested her hand on my shoulder. It didn't feel intrusive. It felt friendly.

I thought the stand looked great, too. "What should we call it?" I asked. "The Pink—"

"—Palace," Tia finished for me. It was just what I had been thinking!

"Let's write it on the sign board. It will face Charlie's house. Since he thought of the Pink Palace name, we should let him share."

Tia nodded, giggled again, and climbed the ladder. I handed her the brush with the black paint on it and she wrote it on the sign board.

"If nothing else, maybe people will wonder what the Pink Palace is and come by," I said.

She climbed back down and we checked our supplies. We had boxes to put the berries in. Our chairs were ready. We slid an empty cashbox under the small counter. Tomorrow I'd bring some change; Papa would give us a little start with that. We had a stash of water bottles.

"We should get up really early and pick," Tia said. "The berries are getting a little ripe, so they are best when they're cool."

I looked at her fingernails. She'd cleaned them well, but there was still an echo of brown under them. Nothing slimy like Mrs. Jenkins' or anything. You could just tell that she'd picked berries. It was okay. My short nails looked like that under the polish, too. I'd been eating strawberries every morning since I got here and helping in the fields my whole life.

"I'll meet you out here early," I said as we walked back to my house to get my bike. I hesitated. "Do you want to see my room?" She'd never seen it before. I hadn't felt like it last time she was over.

"Sure!" she said. We went upstairs.

"This is a quilt I've had since I was a little girl. I know it's kind of tatty, but Grammy made it for me, so I still keep it."

"I know what you mean," she said. "I have a blanket on my bed that my grandmother knit for me. I keep it with me all the time. It was one of the few things I brought with me this year. Knowing I might not go back." Her voice sounded wistful. I'd be really sad if I knew I might not see my Grammy for a long time.

Tia was looking at the framed print of the raspberry vines with the Bible verse, which was still on my windowsill. "Are you a Christian?"

"Yes. Are you?"

Tia nodded. "I go to church in St. John's." She looked like she was going to say something else but then closed her mouth. She touched the picture softly. "It's kind of like us, isn't it?" She read the first two verses out loud. "'I am the true vine, and my Father is the gardener. He cuts off every branch in me that bears no fruit, while every branch that does bear fruit he prunes so that it will be even more fruitful.'"

I nodded. "I think that's why the FFA gave them as gifts. You know, a theme." Papa spent a lot of time pruning the vines, and I guess Tia's dad did, too. They used really sharp shears to slice off the branches. Sometimes I closed my eyes because it looked like it would hurt. Afterward, the vines looked so bare. The next year, though, we had many more berries. I always got too many thorn bites when I tried to prune.

We headed outside. It's kind of hard to talk when you're biking, so we rode pretty much in silence. When we got to the Minit Mart, we each bought a Coke. My voice hadn't been shaking at all anymore, so I indulged.

"Hey, Mark." I handed him a buck and so did Tia.

"Hey, Meg. Who's your friend?"

"Tia."

"Hey, Tia." Mark handed a piece of Dubble Bubble to each of us and we headed toward the beach. It was late in the afternoon, and the beach was only about half full. We picked a spot and spread out a blanket.

"I think most of our business is going to come in

the morning and early afternoon," I said. "Look, all of the Portlanders have left or are getting ready to leave. So they might stop for berries on the way home. The ones who come out just for berries usually come before lunch."

Tia nodded. "Sounds good. We'll get there early and stay late." She looked thoughtful and rolled on her stomach, to match me, and we talked face-to-face. "I have another idea for my portion of the money," Tia continued.

I raised my eyebrows but didn't say anything.

"I know this boy—he's about our age or maybe a little older. He's got to have surgery in September. Our community raised enough money for all of his care, but he wants his mom to come. His mom is in Mexico. There's just not enough money for that, too."

"What a great idea!" I said. "How much do you think it will cost?"

"I don't know. Maybe eight hundred dollars. I'm guessing."

I did the math in my head. Slowly. If she had to earn eight hundred dollars, and I earned that much too, it would be sixteen hundred dollars total that we'd make altogether. Spread over nine weeks, that'd be about $180 every week. That was a lot of berries, especially after we paid for the boxes and stuff. Still—it could be done.

I looked at her, ready to tell her how much I thought we'd have to make. Before I said anything, she nodded. "Sixteen hundred dollars plus expenses," she said. She'd done that really fast. "I'd have to give it in secret because they feel like they've taken enough, even though they are very kind to others."

"I could chip in," I offered.

She shook her head. "No, thank you." Oh great. We were back to the "No, thank you" again. She must have seen the fog pass over my mood.

She reached out and touched my hand. "Everyone is always helping me. I feel grateful for that. But this time I just want to do something on my own. I feel like I have taken enough."

I respected that. I was learning this dance, I think, of respecting the old while introducing the new. Not pushing too much, but just a little. I didn't see yet that I was being pushed, too, in different ways. I would understand that much later.

"I do understand that. I want to buy my shoes and track gear on my own. It's my way of making it mine." We nodded, together, at the same time.

We settled back. I felt, rather than saw, people approach. It was the Portland to Coast team.

They sat down next to us. "Hey," Charlie said. He introduced the others, most of whom I didn't know. One girl I did, though. Natalie. I really looked up to her. She would run this year as a senior for the high school in St. Helens, where I would go if I lived here. She played basketball and danced, and now she led a Brownie troop. Her long brown hair fell gently alongside her face as we chatted for a while. Oh, if I could have a big sister, she'd be it. She was fast, she was smart, she was sweet, she was pretty. Charlie looked at me as if to ask if I'd changed my mind. I shook my head a little. He shrugged and looked away. All of a sudden I didn't care about the Pink Palace anymore. I wanted to be on the team. It seemed that was the story of my life—always wanting to belong to some team, some sport, some family, some town, whatever, and never quite getting there like everyone else seemed to. Why should I give everything up for anyone else? I mean, Tia was a nice girl and all, but it was my summer, too.

"Are you going to the Before the Bridge party?" Charlie asked.

"Of course. My dad might even be home then. I'm not sure," I answered. The Before the Bridge party was for all of the families who lived on Sauvie Island before the bridge was built from Portland, when it was still a true island.

"I didn't know he was coming home. I'm looking forward to seeing him. I know my dad will be, too," Charlie said. "The party is going to be great. Fireworks and barbecue." Most of the others on the team were going to the party, too. Natalie would be there. Maybe at least there I could get to know her a little better.

"Come on, guys," Natalie said. "We'd better get back and do the afternoon run." The team left shortly thereafter. Tia and I didn't have much to talk about, but it was comfortable. I looked at Tia's hair again. I thought how pretty it would be in a Swiss braid or a princess crown. My mom had always braided my hair in pretty patterns before I cut it to shoulder length. I could braid the sides now, if I wanted to, but I'd probably look like Heidi or one of those girls from *The Sound of Music*.

I could have braided Tia's hair for her. I really could have. Part of me wanted to, but the part of me that didn't want her to look beautiful won out and I didn't bring it up at all. I wish I could have. I didn't want to be jealous, but I was.

We started walking toward the bikes. "Yesterday," Tia said, "you called me your friend."

"I did?" I said.

"Yes. You introduced me to Charlie as your friend Tia. You did it again today. Do you really feel that way?"

I nodded. I did. Then I felt like a double dog. I really felt both ways. I wonder if she knew what it cost me to do the berry stand instead of running the Portland to Coast. Maybe she didn't really understand that I finally had a chance to be on a team, a team of friends, a kind of family, doing something good where I could shine. I was the little guy in track at school. My mom and Gary came, so that was cool, but my dad hadn't yet watched me run. I wasn't going to tell Tia what all this meant. But I wasn't ready to forget, either.

When I got home, Grammy and Papa were drinking lemonade and talking over the editorials in the newspaper. It sounded loving. Comfortable. I went into the kitchen and called my mom.

"Hi, Mom."

"Hi, Meggie. I wanted to wait for you to call me, but I've been missing you a lot."

"Me too," I said. I told her about the boy who needed surgery, and how far away his mom was and how she might not be able to come. "I miss you a lot," I said. "As soon as I heard that story today it made me realize how sad I am when we're not together."

"I miss you, too," Mom said, and her voice wobbled like a little bird's.

We talked for a while. "You'll never guess, we're running a berry stand!" I told her about Tia and the berry stand and even Charlie—a little. Before we hung up she tapped three times on the receiver. I tapped four times back. I felt the word *heartache* settle deep inside my rib cage after I set the phone down and stood there for a minute or two.

Later that night Papa huffed up the stairs. "I know you're too old to need tucking in, but I can kiss a girl good-night, you know." Papa smooched my cheek, and I hugged him. It was quiet. I lay in bed, thinking.

I'd been asking to hear from God, even when I was in Seattle. Everyone always talked about how I was supposed to be personal with Him, but I had the hardest time getting there. How do you do that? No one ever tells you that part. *God, I thought I'd heard you in church, calling me softly, tenderly, come home. I also felt a squeeze on my heart when Tia read the passage about the vines. Was that you?* My dad must have studied that passage when he got the frame or he wouldn't have kept it. Maybe my dad kept it for me. Maybe I could learn God's language after all. I'd start with John 15 and take it from there.

When I was smaller, Papa used to tell me stories every night before I got tucked in. Lots of them were farm stories, of course. One of them was about some wild vines that took over a farm. A man carefully cultivated his raspberry patch, placing only plants that would grow sweet and enduring fruit. One day, though, he realized there were a few blackberry vines, which are really weeds, in his garden.

That farmer was too busy, though. He hadn't realized how fast blackberry vines grow. Soon they took over everything else, choking out the good fruit and ruining the whole farm. "Do you know what those vines are like?" Papa asked me. No, I'd said. "Anger, selfishness, jealousy, and fear." Then he kissed me and went downstairs. I understood what Papa was saying, but I also understood the other farmer. Sometimes people don't have the will or desire to chop out all those tough vines of anger and jealousy and fear. It's hard to do. And the thorns bite.

CHAPTER FIVE

The rest of that week and the whole next week were an unqualified disaster. No joking. The first day Tia and I hauled ourselves out of bed at an hour when even the birds were still dreaming. We knelt down by the strawberry mounds and picked in silence. Each of us had flat boxes to fill and bring back to the shack, and then we'd go back for more. I thought about that kneeling stuff. Tia had told me that at her church they kneel for a lot of things. There are little kneelers that flip out from the pew ahead of them, and at different times everyone in church would kneel. I thought the kneeling part was cool. I mean, He is God, after all. I'd kneel.

Picking strawberries is hot, hard work. Your knees hurt and they get dirty. Your back hurts. The sun beats down on you the second it ascends. You have to pick the berries with their little green elf hat on, just right. One good thing is you get to eat all the fresh berries you want. There's nothing like eating something minutes after it was picked. When we eat anything in the summer it's totally fresh. Grammy is a stickler for that. When we make corn on the cob, she gets the water boiling before we even pick the corn. I wanted these berries to be fresh. I wanted a good reputation. Tia was in total agreement. We wanted to succeed.

After all that kneeling and plucking we had filled about a dozen boxes with berries. "I figure one of us can run out and pick some more really fast if we get down to two or three boxes," I said. "That way we won't pick too many."

"I'm a really fast picker," Tia said.

She was, and I was, too.

We sat at the Pink Palace and waited. And waited. We were right on the road—but way *down* the road. One car came by—this old guy who was a friend of Grammy and Papa's. It was nice that he bought some berries, but I know he has berries of his own, so it was flat-out charity. I guess I didn't care much for flat-out charity, either. Mrs. Richards came over. "I wanted to try some of your grandpa's new hybrids," she said. "The old coot won't let me taste them till the university comes to test in a day or two, so I thought I'd sneak over and buy what you have instead."

Tia and I gladly sold her two boxes. I wondered if Charlie would be eating strawberry shortcake from my farm for dessert. Later we had six whole boxes of berries left. Berries that had to either be eaten, frozen, or pitched by the next day.

"We're not doing too well," Tia said.

"You have a talent for speaking the obvious," I kidded her, and she smiled.

We brought the berries into the house and went swimming for the afternoon. Later Tia came home with me. Grammy was upstairs on the phone, chatting. I could hear her.

"I wish I knew how to make strawberry shortcake," I said. "Normally I just buy pound cake at the store and put some canned whipped cream on it."

"I can teach you," Tia said. "I make chocolate cake that we can put the leftover strawberries on. Chocolate started in Mexico, you know."

"No, I didn't know that. Can you really make it? Do you think we have everything?"

"Should I look?" she asked. I nodded. Tia opened

the cupboards with ease; it looked like she'd been through them before. "My *abuela,* my grandmother, lets me cook a lot. She doesn't like to. There's a lot of science involved in cooking. I love that."

"Grammy's always trying to teach me how to bake, but I'm not too good." I hoped Grammy wouldn't mind that we were whipping this stuff up. I'd have to make sure it was good and clean afterward. "I'd like to make something homemade for my dad when he comes home, though. I've only made cookies before."

Tia whipped the cakes up in no time at all. She showed me how to whisk eggs into a froth. Baking lesson number one!

After we pulled the cakes from the oven, Tia glanced at the clock on the wall. "I'd better go. Dinner together is very important to my dad, and he'll be mad if I'm late."

I made sure she took half of the berries and the cake. I hoped she had some whipping cream at home.

"Meg! This is delicious," Papa said as he dug into the cake after dinner. "Chocolate was a great idea."

"Tia made it," I said. "Shortcakes were my idea, though."

"Oh, well, good teamwork. How did sales go?"

"Not good," I had to admit. I filled them in on the bad news.

"Tomorrow's another day," Grammy said. "Maybe

put some balloons out there. I'll see if I have some in the party box." Grammy really wanted this to work. And we were having fun because we were getting to know each other and our friendship was growing.

The second week wasn't much better. Actually, it was worse, because it was hotter than lizard feet and we still had no sales. We even had balloons that Grammy put out. At least once a day Charlie and Natalie and the team went jogging by in matching T-shirts, shorts, and caps, training for the Portland to Coast. Most of the time they waved at both of us. Charlie, to his credit, didn't ask how many berries we were selling. He could see that the only things buzzing around the Pink Palace were crows.

"When should we quit?" Tia asked.

I shook my head. "I don't know. When you have a real job you have to give them two weeks' notice before you can quit and still hold your head up. I suppose two weeks is a good amount of time. What do you think?"

"I agree," she said. We sat down again. And waited.

It would be the Fourth of July soon. Raspberries would be in, and the strawberries were going bad.

"After church I talked to the family of the boy with the surgery, Daniel," Tia said one day as we sat in the shade waiting for customers to appear out of nowhere. "He's so glad he's going to get better. I think he still misses his mom, though. He used the last of his phone cards to call her. It costs a lot."

"I'm sorry. I was hoping we could make more than this," I said. I shook the cashbox, where a few lonely coins cowered under a stray bill or two.

"I should have given him my phone card, but I want to save it to call my abuela instead," Tia said.

I liked her even better then.

The week before the Fourth of July was week number two, the one before our quitting deadline. The berries were starting to show their age a little, but they were still good. Mr. Ramos came over and helped us arrange the berries in the box so they looked their most appetizing. Then he went back to the barn, where he was supervising the field workers who were gathering fruit to sell to jam processors. That's where most of Grammy and Papa's money came from. Selling fruit to companies. Good thing, too, or they'd starve trying to sell it to customers way out here.

"Have you noticed that the cars seem to turn off before they come down here?" Tia asked. "Like they're heading to Reeder Beach or around the other side of the Island to that really big farm that has ponies and stuff."

"Maybe Charlie was right," I answered. "We *are* too far down the road."

The past few days when the team had run by in training, there was someone missing. I didn't know who it was—didn't remember the person from the lineup on the other days. But there was definitely an open slot. I watched them sweat and get faster and laugh and call out encouragement to one another. I wondered if someone was on vacation or sick or had dropped out. I wished I were running, too.

In spite of our neatly arranged berries, we packed up at the end of the day with two boxes left. We'd made a grand total of one hundred dollars for all of the strawberry sales. I didn't even want to figure out what that came to per hour for the whole week. Probably twenty-five cents each. We could have been biking, shopping, going to the library or to town or to the beach, or running. A million other things besides this. And there still was no money for a flight from Mexico for Daniel's mom. Or for quality track shoes for me.

"Want to go biking?" I asked Tia.

"Sure," she said. She ran home to wash the berry juice off of her hands and get on a fresh T-shirt. It was kind of weird that she'd never invited me over to her house even though she'd been to my house a lot. I wondered if her mom didn't like me or if they were embarrassed somehow. I might work up the courage to ask her. I didn't want to freak her out, though, or be pushy. When she came back, she handed me a bandanna. "I have two of these. Do you want one? It's hot out."

"Sure!" I tied one around my hair, and she did, too, so we matched. We both smiled.

"Where should we go?" I asked.

"I don't feel like the beach today. How about you?" she said.

I didn't really feel like it, either. "I know," I said. "Follow me."

We took off up the road the other direction, away from town and deeper into the territory that was the wildlife preserve. It got even quieter except for the sound of the birds. When we had gone long enough that the road was almost ready to give up, I pulled to the side. "Come on."

"Where are we going?" Tia leaned her bike down next to mine.

"You'll see." We waded through the marshes, the grass scratching at our calves. I knew what I was looking for, and it was still there, perched in an old tree. A room with slatted boards to peek through and let the breeze in. Most of the boards were loose. It looked like the Pink Palace had before Mr. Ramos tightened the boards, only this was about twenty feet up.

"Is this the tree house you and your dad built?" Tia asked.

"Yeah, one summer a while ago," I said, more softly than I'd planned. It kind of made me sad to see the old place in such bad shape. Tia's dad had helped tighten the boards on the shack. Maybe my dad could help fix this up soon. I'd have to ask him.

Tia was inspecting some grass and bugs—science

again. "Hey, come on!" I called.

We crawled up the tree, one foot after another gripping the boards that Dad had nailed in to use as a ladder. When we got up there, it was still pretty firm. Firm enough to hold two girls, anyway.

I looked over the island from that point, the fields of berries, the other stands. "It's not working," I said.

"What do you mean? The berry stand?"

I nodded. "No one is coming down the road. Charlie was right. I hate to admit that, but it's true."

"It does seem like a waste of time," Tia said. "We could be doing a lot of other things. I haven't even been to visit my cousins in St. John's or anything. I think they're having a lot of fun."

"I haven't been running too much, either," I said. "We gave it two weeks." We sat there in the silence, the day a deep quiet except for the buzz and hiccup of the marsh bugs, a sound only a hot summer afternoon can make.

"Are you glad your dad is coming home?" Tia asked.

"Yes. But I kind of wish my mom was here, too," I said. "I wish my parents hadn't divorced. Even though Gary is an awesome Christian guy, it's not the same. And I don't know if I want this baby or not. I kind of wish the whole deal would go away. But then, I kind of want a brother or a sister. I don't know."

Tia held the silence a long time before answering. "When Grammy first told me that you were coming,

I thought you would have a perfect life. You have money, two houses to live in, and your grandparents near you. You have your dad coming back."

I shook my head hard and shifted position. Several of the boards creaked. "Uh-oh, Tia." I stood up carefully. "Let's climb down. We'll have real problems if we crash out of this tree. Bigger problems than the rotting already-picked, not-yet-sold berries at the Pink Palace."

Tia went down first, and I followed. "I have an idea of what we can do with the soft berries," she said. I looked at her with surprise. "If we can go to your house for a little while, I'll show you what I mean," she said.

I let her lead the way.

Grammy was upstairs because her hair was in rollers and she never lets anyone see that. Papa was watching TV. We brought the boxes of berries into the kitchen.

"Do you have a blender?" Tia asked.

I nodded and opened the lazy Susan cabinet. I pulled out a blender that looked like it had been assembled the year man first landed on the moon. "I hope it still works."

Tia got out the milk and sugar. I cut the berries, which dyed my nails red. I smiled. Next time Charlie came by I was going to apply some nice red berry juice to my lips. We tossed the berries into the blender and Tia whipped it up. I poured a glassful for each of us. It was good, really good, especially since the berries were fresh.

I was fussing in the spice cupboard, trying to make room for the sugar to go back, when I came across the chocolate syrup. "Hey! What would happen if we put this in there? Or even ice cream?"

"I don't know!" Tia said. "Let's try." She squirted some into the blender.

I have to admit, it was one of my better moments. Maybe I *could* be a cook after all. That was an encouraging thought. We frothed it up and it was fantastic—like chocolate strawberry shortcake in a glass.

"Let's do one more batch," Tia said. She poured all of the ingredients in and turned the blender on. Except this time she hadn't put the lid on tightly enough. All of a sudden smoothie flew all over the kitchen ceiling. Strawberry strings were hanging from the ceiling fan—and in my hair.

I saw the horror in Tia's eyes.

"Oh no! What a mess! What shall we do?!" she cried.

I wanted her to feel okay, not awkward, not like she'd done something wrong. "It's okay," I said, picking a chunk out of my hair. "I *am* a strawberry blonde, after all."

She cracked a smile and I let my breath out. The tension passed and now we laughed together.

I grabbed every single dish towel out of the drawer. "Pray like crazy that Grammy's hair isn't set yet and that Papa is totally into his show!"

We stood on chairs and wiped the walls and ceiling as best we could with water and lemon dish soap. Tia picked a berry clump off of her shirt. "New design," she joked. I wrapped a towel over my head and pretended to back away from her. She laughed harder.

Ten minutes later we stopped to breathe again and inspect the room. "I think we got it all," I said. I ran the heap of towels back into the laundry room. I'd wash them when Grammy and Papa were at the Grange meeting that night.

"We got it all! I'd better get back for dinner, Meg. You know my dad," Tia said. I did understand him better now. And liked him more.

I showed her how to do a high five and she walked toward the back acreage. I cleaned a last speck off of the window, and as I did I saw the team run by. Charlie was in front, but I knew they took turns. *The team*, that's how I thought of them.

After Grammy and Papa left for the Before the Bridge party meeting at the Grange—a kind of country community hall—I started the washer. If I was careful, I could get them cleaned and folded before they got back. Grammy was very picky about neatness.

I sat down and ate a bowl of tomato soup with saltine crackers. The frogs were out, but there were other sounds, too. The sound of Tia's family eating dinner together and laughing and chattering in Spanish washed across the yard. I peeked out the window. They looked so happy. Talk about perfect. I was lonely and my soup was getting cold. Where was my mom? My dad?

I sat down at the table again, alone, and licked my saltine. It reminded me of the taste of tears trickling down my face. I put my bowl and spoon away and pulled out my phone card. I'd try my dad again. I'd already tried once right before I came to the Island, but I'd gotten his executive officer, who offered to take a message for him. Maybe I could ask Dad if we could fix the fort when he got home. Yes!

"Hello, you've reached the voice mail of Colonel Paul West. I'm in the field, so please dial my executive officer if this business needs to be attended to immediately. Thank you."

I didn't leave a message. I didn't want his executive officer. I wanted my dad. On the way into the laundry room, I pitched the phone card into the trash. It seemed like Dad never took my calls. Maybe God wasn't taking them, either, or else He'd fix this mess for me. I hadn't heard from Him in a long time, either, even though I'd asked to.

When I got up to my room, I turned the framed picture of the berry fields and the verses against the wall. I was tempted to shove it back under the bed, but even though I was mad, I couldn't do that. By the end of the evening, I'd decided about the berry booth. I'd tell Tia in the morning.

The teary taste of those saltines reminded me. One time last year I went to the movies with a couple of friends. I had a speck of something in my contact. If I'd taken the contact out, I wouldn't have been able to see the movie. It hurt being in there, though. I had no contact solution. I didn't want to make a fuss and upset anyone, but I also didn't want to hurt anymore. Partway through the movie someone really wonderful died and I started to cry, just a little. After a while the tears washed that speck right out of my eye.

CHAPTER SIX

I went to Tia's house right away in
the morning, as I'd planned. We'd agreed
ahead of time that since we weren't going to
pick berries we could sleep in a bit. Mr.
Ramos was home with Pablo, but Tia and her
mom had gone to St. John's, Mr. Ramos said.

Pablo met me at the door. "Licorice?" he
asked. I shook my head no. I didn't carry it
with me *all* the time! He looked so disappointed.

"Want to play soccer?" I asked.

He nodded his head. "Okay!" He kicked his ball to me and I kicked it back. He was actually pretty good for a little tyke, and fast.

"You could be a runner someday, kid," I said.

"Nah," he said. "I like soccer." He bopped the ball with his head and then ran across the field. Mr. Ramos was tinkering on another tractor but kept one eye on his son. It was amazing. Papa had some really old equipment, but it seemed to run better than ever this year. I followed Pablo farther out in the field, and we kicked the ball back and forth. I had always liked soccer, too, but the elite soccer teams in my area played year round and I was always gone all summer. If I stayed in one place for a while, I might be able to pick it back up. I wondered if they had good year-round teams here that I could join if I lived here. I bet they did. I'd have to ask someone, maybe Natalie.

I kicked the ball to Pablo, and he powed it back to me. I blocked and the ball started back toward him. When he dove for it, he fell instead. "Ow!" Pablo tumbled to the ground, face first.

"Are you okay?" I ran toward him and saw Mr. Ramos coming, too. I knelt down to pick him up and he smiled. He stood up, a little shaky. I spotted the root that he had tripped over, still half in the ground and half out. "Let's get it!" I said to him. I tugged and groaned and moaned. "No more life for you, you nasty root. Knocking down the great soccer player

Pablo Ramos. For that you will pay!" By the time I had tugged it out and snapped it in half, Pablo was laughing. Mr. Ramos laughed, too. Pablo tugged a clean sheet off of the line and wiped the dirt from his mouth. "Uh-oh, your mother is going to kill you!" I said. I rolled him up in the sheet and carried him back to the house.

"I'm a burrito!" he said, laughing.

"A very cute burrito," I told him. I deposited him on his front porch and unwrapped him. "Tell your sister to come over to my house when she gets home, okay?"

"Okay," he agreed. Then he raced off to help his dad with the tractor.

When I got back to the house, Grammy was puttering in the kitchen. I noticed that the dish towels were folded and placed back in the drawer. Oh! I'd forgotten to finish the load last night. Also, I saw her wiping down the appliances.

"Was Tia home?" Grammy asked. She wiped some smoothie goo from the top of the cupboards and smiled at me. She said nothing, but I knew she knew.

I smiled back. "Nope. Gone to St. John's for the day, I think."

"I think she has a lot of cousins there," Grammy said. "Have you decided what you're going to do about the stand?" Grammy's smile melted away and her eyes looked a little older.

"I think so," I said. I couldn't blame Tia for

wanting to spend some time with her cousins and friends if we weren't doing berries. I peeked out the window. No one was running by right now. Maybe they'd practice later on this week. It was getting hot out. Running at night or early morning was a better idea.

"I fished this out of the garbage this morning." Grammy held out the phone card to me.

"Oh. Thanks," I said.

"Your dad called while you were gone this morning."

"He did?" My eyes filled with tears. "I missed him?" Sometimes he couldn't call for days or weeks if he was in the field.

"He said he'll call back in an hour. You might want to stick around."

You bet I did. I twiddled around doing nothing, arranging and rearranging my hair gear in a Caboodles box. Finally the phone rang.

"Hi, Dad?" I answered the phone. I'm glad it was him. Grammy and Papa don't believe in caller ID.

"Hi, sugar," he said. "How is my best and only girl?"

"I'm great. Are you coming home?"

"I am. I will be there very soon. In time for the Before the Bridge party, for sure. I'm eager to see Papa's new berries. And there's a certain girl I'm waiting to spend time with."

I smiled, and I could tell it shone in my voice.

"Papa froze some berries for you," I said. "So you could taste them at their peak."

"I have some surprises for you. What would you like to do? Eat out? Go shopping?"

"Yeah. And talk. We'll sit on the porch. We can buy you your own chair. Yeah! That's what we'll do. Also, Dad?"

"Yes?"

"Can we fix up the tree fort? My friend and I went there yesterday and it's getting kind of rickety."

"Yes, sugar, we'll fix it up and more. We can talk when I get home. Okay?"

We talked for another couple of minutes, and then Dad signed off because it was getting close to bedtime in Germany even though it was barely lunchtime on Sauvie Island. It was okay, though. He'd be home soon.

I love my mom a lot. But I kind of wanted to see what it would be like to have my dad come running when I fell down, or laugh with me at the dinner table, or help me work on projects. I had never had that before, like normal kids have.

After I talked with Dad, I went back up to my room. I turned the little plaque face up again and dusted it off. It had belonged to Dad, after all. I read the next couple of verses. *Remain in me, and I will remain in you. No branch can bear fruit by itself; it must remain in the vine. Neither can you bear fruit unless you remain in me. I am the vine; you are the branches. If a*

man *remains in me and I in him, he will bear much fruit;*
apart from me you can do nothing."

Help me, Lord. I wanted to be fruitful and good
and do right things. I wanted to remain in Him, and
Him in me. I wanted to produce much fruit so my
life could have meaning. Is that what the verses
meant?

Most especially, though, I didn't want Him to stop
talking to me.

A little later on Tia came over. "Hi!" she called
through the screen door. She could see me sitting on
the living room floor reading.

I leaped up. "Hi! Guess what, my dad called. He's
going to help us fix up the tree fort."

"That's really good. Hey—I can't stay long
because I have to help my mom out. She and my dad
want to know if you can come over for dinner
tonight."

"I'll ask Grammy!" I dashed upstairs, where
Grammy was chatting on the phone. When she saw
me she put her hand over the mouthpiece.

"Can I eat at Tia's tonight?" I whispered. She
smiled and nodded. I ran back downstairs.

"We're on!" I said. Tia smiled and headed home.
I ran back to my room and dug through my closet,
flinging aside outfit after outfit. What should I wear?
And hey! Did her mom speak English? I didn't think
so. Maybe I'd better practice a few Spanish phrases. I
tracked down the Spanish phrase book Grammy kept

in the phonebook drawer for when she needed to talk with the field workers. I had to dig to find it. Grammy didn't use it much now that Mr. Ramos was supervising the workers. That gave Grammy time to host game night with her friends and chat on the phone.

I paged through the book. "I have a stomach-ache." Ah, no, I didn't think that would work. "Can you direct me to a police officer?" No again. "What time does the bakery open?" No.

Finally I found two that would work. *Gracias para la cena.* "Thank you for dinner." *Usted tiene un hogar encantador.* "You have a lovely home." That oughta do it.

Later that evening I sat down at the kitchen table, waiting to head over. I snapped and unsnapped my star clips and rearranged them. I wore my new jeans and a shirt. I wondered if Tia was the kind of friend who would tell you if you had a ball of earwax or if your hair looked goofy. Better to hear it from a friend than a stranger.

"It's really an honor to be invited over to their home for dinner," Papa said. "In their culture, they don't make fast friends like we do. Their friendships are more carefully given—but more likely to last."

I remembered the look Mr. Ramos had when he saw me rolling up Pablo. I know that Tia understood she was my friend. I felt a little better now about her not inviting me over earlier. "I understand," I answered. "I feel honored to be accepted and invited as a friend. I hope I can repay the favor."

"Oh, I almost forgot!" I ran upstairs and got the small envelope that held a surprise I'd planned for Tia and slid it into my purse.

A few minutes later it was time. I started walking through the yard, praying in my head that God would help me do what needed to be done with the berry stand. I heard a noise and jumped. No one should be out here right now!

"Hey, it's just me." Charlie came out of our barn. It spooked me.

"What are you doing here?" I asked.

"Returning some equipment that my dad borrowed." He looked at me a little longer. I don't think he was used to seeing me in anything except running shorts and T-shirts. He didn't say I looked nice, but I could tell he was thinking it. It's just the kind of thing a girl knows. I was glad that Tia wasn't there. Oh boy, there it was again. Jealousy. *Please, God, take that away.*

Chop out that vine, I heard in my heart. I jumped, startled to hear His voice so clearly even though I'd been asking to.

I will, I answered.

"Where are you going?" Charlie asked.

"To Tia's for dinner. I'd better get going," I said.

He nodded and headed home. He turned around once to look back at me. I saw him out of the corner of my eye, but I didn't flick my head—not even half an inch. So he didn't know that I'd noticed him looking back at me.

I didn't have to make it all the way to Tia's door before I smelled dinner. Oh boy. I love Mexican food. I could smell the hot spices, the chorizo, everything. I knocked on the door, just a little.

Pablo opened the door. "Licorice?" he asked.

"Hello to you, too," I said. I reached into my purse and drew out a little Baggie of licorice. He smiled and ran back toward his bedroom.

Tia and I sat on the small couch in the living room. Over the back of it was a knitted afghan. I can't exactly explain the mix of emotions I felt when I saw what was on the table next to the couch. Sadness, disappointment, happiness, and surprise all at once. I hope that no one else saw how I looked. On the table, right next to the couch, were strings. Knitted strings, exactly like the one wrapped around my flower posy.

My secret anonymous flowers hadn't been from Charlie. They'd been from Tia.

Tia's mom came into the room and welcomed us into the kitchen. A little table was set up in the tidy room. Beautiful embroidered white curtains hung at each window. "How pretty," I managed to say, still recovering from the shock I'd just had.

"My abuela and my mother sew and knit," Tia said. "I don't."

"I do," I said. "I love to knit." Tia turned and told her mother. Her mother smiled at me. It felt kind of cool. I mean, Grammy and Tia cooked, but I knit, just like her mom and abuela. It seemed as good of a time as any to try out my first Spanish phrase. "Usted tiene un hogar encantador."

"Oh! Bueno, gracias," her mother answered. She called Tia's dad and brother in and had me repeat the phrase, and then they all clapped for me. It felt really good. I felt, right away, like I belonged.

An hour later, overstuffed with chicken tamales, rice, beans, and flan, Tia and I headed to her room. I saw the blanket on her bed, the one her grandma had made.

We sat down on the floor together. "Are you excited that your dad is coming home?" she asked.

"Very. He doesn't always get leave in the summer, when I'm here. He's up for advancement. When you get to be at his rank in the army, either you get promoted or you retire. He'll probably go up to Fort Lewis in Seattle for a little while when he's here and find out for sure. If he retires, he'll come back to live on Sauvie Island and help Papa run the farm. I could stay and live with him if I wanted. I love my mom and Gary. But I sure would like to spend more time with my dad, too. You don't know how lucky you are to see your dad all the time."

"I don't, though, remember? Lots of times I'm in Mexico and he's here."

"I never thought about that," I said. I hadn't. I *had* thought about the fact that if my dad helped Papa run the farm, Tia's dad would not be necessary anymore. One of us could live here all year. But not both of us.

"What should we do about the berries?" I asked. "The strawberries are all ripe or almost overripe. Soon it will be time for raspberries. The real problem is, no one is coming to the Pink Palace."

"I know. Should we close it down?"

"What else can we do? I don't want to waste the whole summer and neither do you. I'm sorry we couldn't make it work; I really wanted to be successful. To prove to old Charlie that we could make it go. To make Grammy proud, and the dads, yours and mine. I'm also sorry we couldn't help your friend with the money. And buy my shoes."

"Me too," Tia said. "I saw that boy, Daniel, today in St. John's. I was at my cousin's house. I was telling them all about that smoothie you made last night. Everyone wished they could have tried one. I said maybe we'd make one for them next time they came."

I don't think either of us had the idea first, because when I looked at her I could see that she had the idea all of a sudden, too. "We could sell smoothies," I said. "No one else is doing that. I bet we could charge like three dollars each for them."

"Where would we get the supplies? What would we need?" Her eyes shone.

"Blenders. Cups. Ice. Fruit. Sugar. Any extra ingredients like maybe ice cream or yogurt." I smiled big, real big.

"How much would all of that cost?" Tia asked. I could see she wanted to do it. I did, too. All of a sudden the challenge became real. All at once we became a team of our own. It wasn't about me. It wasn't about her. It was about us.

"I don't know. Maybe a hundred dollars," I said.

"We have a hundred dollars, if we're willing to risk it. I'd like the booth to be a success before your dad comes home. So he's proud of you," she said. I warmed. I felt certain that she *was* the kind of friend who would tell you, privately, about the earwax.

"I want to make the money for your friend," I said. "And to make *your* dad proud of you, too. His little businesswoman." She giggled.

For the rest of the evening we brainstormed our plan. Well, I brainstormed, really, and Tia wrote it all down and made sense of the random plans I tossed out. I was the artistic one, after all. She was precise. One time she caught Pablo listening at the door and yelled at him, in Spanish, to get away. I liked her even more.

On the way out I handed her the envelope. "Take this," I said. It was my phone card. My dad would be home soon, so I wouldn't need it anymore. She could call her abuela, since it might be months before she saw her.

"No, no," she said. She didn't look happy, like I thought she would. When I finally explained that I couldn't use it anymore, she took it and softened a little, like just-ripe berries, and said thank-you. I know it had to do with what she told me at Reeder Beach. She had given me the flower posy, but in secret. She wanted to give her gift for her friend's mother in secret. Charity was a no-no.

The moon was so bright it seemed to send shafts of light down to the earth and hold hands with the trees themselves. I walked through the field and looked at the Richardses' place in the distance. I sighed. It was kind of hard, knowing that Charlie hadn't given me the flowers. It would have been my first gift from a boy. But he had looked at me a little differently tonight. Hadn't he? Or was I imagining that? Only time would tell, as my mother would say. Did the Lord give us the idea about the smoothies, or had we imagined that on our own? Only time would tell.

One day when I was a little girl, Grammy sat outside on the porch with me late into the night. I had helped her clean all the rooms before a party, so my reward was to stay up till the partygoers had gone home. We sat out on the porch, and the moon was full and bright. Did you know, she asked me, that the June full moon is called the Strawberry Moon? For us it means strawberry season is almost over and raspberry season is about to begin. You never could tell, from one year to the next, what the berry harvest would be. Sometimes you would expect it to be great and all of a sudden a disaster would happen—too much rain, too many bugs—and all would be lost. You'd have to start over. But sometimes the sun was better than you'd hoped it would be and the fields were healthy and the birds and bugs stayed away for reasons only God himself knew.

Sometimes things came crashing down, but sometimes they worked out better that you could have hoped. Only time would tell.

CHAPTER SEVEN

E ven a brainstormer like me
realized you have to have a plan. So
we decided to plan the next day or two and
make our big push over the Fourth of July
weekend. Tia didn't know too much about
the Fourth of July.

"It's a national holiday," I explained. "To
celebrate when our country began its fight for
freedom from the British. We have fireworks
and parties, and lots of people come to the

beach because everyone has vacation time."

"Ah, like Cinco de Mayo," she said. "I have been here for a couple of those holidays."

"Will you be sad to be an American and not a Mexican if you stay here?" I asked.

"I can be both," she said. "There is a part of me that will always be a Mexican. There is a part of me that is eager to be an American. I'll be a Mexican-American. A blend of two very good things."

I thought about that, a lot. I guess, with my family, I was a blend of two very good things, too. There was my mom and Gary—and Baby—and I was going to be a big sister. Then there was my dad, who was finally coming home. I belonged both places, but I couldn't live split in two.

Grammy was so psyched that we weren't abandoning the booth that she let me out of my chores for a couple of days while we planned for the new smoothie stand. Papa pshawed the idea that we could make it work at all. He was a doubter. Grammy chased him out to the barn again. The U of O people had come and taken his berry samples, so he was tinkering on something new. Or at least he pretended he was so he could keep away from Grammy's broom handle.

Tia and I camped out at the tree house to plan. We were careful not to tip the fragile house before Dad and I could tighten it up. I brought some paper and pens to help us keep track.

"What will we need?"

I wrote as Tia talked. "Cups. Ice. Crushed ice would be better, don't you think?" The sunlight slit in through the slats in the walls. I squinted and saw *Meg + Dad were here* written in my childish handwriting. I caught my breath, missing my dad again. Then I felt disloyal and missed my mom, and Gary, too. Sometimes it was all too much to handle. I got back to the smoothies.

"We have the berries," I said. "The strawberries will be good for a while—for smoothies anyway, since they're soft. Then what—raspberry smoothies?"

"Good! Very good!" Tia said. "We can add yogurt to them to make them even healthier. They won't have that yummy chocolate flavor, though."

"Why not?" I asked. "Couldn't we call it 'Dark Chocolate Raspberry Delight' or something? They could order it with or without chocolate."

"*Sí*, we could." We went through the rest of the list. We'd need to rent a commercial blender. Papa could run an extension cord from the barn to the shack for us. Because we worked on a farm, we wouldn't need a food handler's license, which was great, because who had time for that? We had two months to make sixteen hundred dollars. That was gobs of dough.

"Have you ever made money like that?" I asked Tia as we carefully climbed down out of the tree house. A board fell off of the house and almost conked me on the head.

"Are you okay?" she asked.

I nodded. No more tree house till Dad came home. We started walking home, the grass whispering against our legs.

"I've never made money like that," she said. "My dad didn't even have steady work for a long time. How about you?"

I shook my head. "No. I baby-sat a few times. I even went to the certification course—you know, where they make you place a rubber baby on the floor and pretend to breathe into his mouth?"

"What else did you learn?"

"Oh, how to pack a baby-sitting bag. You know— take some safe toys, a pad of paper to write down instructions, safety tips, all that."

"Fun! Did you get to do much?"

I shook my head. "I watched the boy next door for a while, but he told his mother I was a bad baby-sitter and mean and she never asked me back."

"Why did he say that?" Tia asked.

"I wouldn't let him color on the walls, I guess, I don't know. But his mom never asked me back, so I just kind of stuck my bag into the closet and figured baby-sitting wasn't for me." It had hurt. I didn't say that, though. I never dragged the bag out again.

We got back to my house and showed Grammy our list of stuff.

She checked it all off and made a call. "You can go to the Quinns' place and get most of this. They have a farm supply. I know Rob Quinn will help you out. I'll get the cups, lids, chocolate syrup, and yogurt at the warehouse store when I go this afternoon. I'd take you girls with me, but you'd best get on to Rob's and see what he can supply. You'll have to pay me for the supplies, of course," she said with a twinkle. She meant it, though. Grammy was no soft touch.

We rode bikes to the Quinns' farm. Rob Quinn processed a lot of his own fruit, so he had equipment and supplies that most of us didn't. He loaded up a large blender and an ice chest into his ancient Ford truck and putt-putted back to the shack. "I'll have them bring by some ice when they drop mine off," he said. "No charge for the equipment, but you'll have to pay for the ice."

"No, we'll pay you to rent the equipment," I said.

"Nope," Mr. Quinn said. "It'll make your Grammy mad if you don't and that'll tickle me." He laughed out loud, and it made me and Tia laugh, too. It would get Grammy. "Say, look here," he said. He held out a large box of small plastic cups. "I used to give jam samples away in these, but I don't do that much anymore. I don't suppose you girls would be interested in these, would you?"

We hadn't thought of giving smoothies away. I mean, wouldn't that defeat the purpose?

"People always bought jam when I showed 'em, with their taste buds, how very good it was," Mr. Quinn said.

I nodded. Of course! Tia looked uncertain, but I smiled at her to show her that it would be okay. Mr. Quinn drove away, and we took the large box of small cups home.

When Grammy came home later, we told her about Mr. Quinn. "Oh, that man," she said. "He's been bugging me for forty-five years because I married Papa instead of him."

Tia looked at me and I looked at Tia. We both looked at Grammy. Grammy had boys chasing her when she was young? It seemed hard to believe. What was worse was the thought that I might actually look like Grammy in sixty years. I shook off the thought of myself in rollers and a housedress sitting on padded chairs and eating garlic pretzel mix while I played games with my old lady friends. Scary.

We brought all the ingredients out to the shed and changed our sign again so it said, "Pink Palace—Delicious, Cool Fruit Smoothies." After it was just so, I walked Tia home. When we got closer, Pablo came running up. "Licorice?" he asked. I knew he would. It warmed me. I pulled out a Baggie from my pack. Tia picked him up and ran her fingers through his hair, scolding him in Spanish. She set him back down and he ran away, giggling.

"I told him how rude it was that he asked for my

friend before asking for me," she said. She looked at me and smiled. "In Mexico, you would have used your baby-sitting bag quite a bit. I think that little neighbor boy didn't know what he was missing."

I think it was the first compliment she'd paid me. It meant a lot. We'd come pretty far from the crabby-look days we'd started off with. We agreed to meet at the shack early the next morning to meet the ice man and go from there.

I walked home thinking about what she'd said. Pablo was a good kid. I wouldn't mind kicking the soccer ball with him every day or feeding him licorice or walking him to school.

I sat out in the fields. The strawberries were dying. The raspberries were springing to life, and the air was thick with the smell of both—the syrupy sweetness of almost-death and the lighter sweetness of life.

"What's up?" Charlie walked across the field and sat next to me. I felt his nearness in a way I hadn't felt from a boy before, like the warmth from his arms was traveling across the way to my arms without them even touching.

"Thinking," I said.

"About your berry stand?" I waited for the sting, the joke, but none came. So I decided to be honest.

"Yeah. We're not going to sell berries anymore."

"Hey, I'm sorry. I'm really sorry you missed your chance to be on the team, too. I mean, if anyone drops off I'll let you know."

I almost got the feeling he was hoping someone would. "No one is going to drop off now," I said. Besides, that wasn't the point.

"You'd need new shoes, though." He gestured to mine. "Those are absolute dogs."

I wrinkled my nose. "I know. But I couldn't be on the team anyway. We're opening a smoothie stand. Tia and I are."

A slow smile spread across his face. "Cool! That might just work! What a great idea. Who thought of that?"

"We both did," I said a little too quickly.

"That Tia seems like a nice girl."

"She is," I said. "But she doesn't run." I could almost hate myself for doing that—jumping right in to point out something bad about her. My shoes were dogs. So was I. But I didn't take it back.

Charlie looked at me funny. "I know she doesn't run." He stood up. "Well, I'll see you around. Good luck with the smoothies. I hope you succeed. I think you can do it."

He sauntered off across the field to his house. I waited till he was far off, so he wouldn't think I was following him, and then I went to the raspberry canes and popped a few raspberries into my mouth.

Yum. Perfect. I felt more determined than ever to make this smoothie thing work. My dad would be home soon. My dad always got everything right. He got promoted. He got good grades. His shoes were always clean, for goodness' sake! But he hadn't made the stand work. I could. And he'd be proud of me. In just a few days, practically, he'd be here.

The next morning Tia and I met the ice man and—yes! He brought crushed ice.

We shut the ice chest so the ice would stay cold and put the yogurt in there, too. It wouldn't matter if it got a little too cool. It would just make the smoothies thicker. On a shelf on the back wall Tia had set out all the bottles of chocolate syrup right in a row, lined up like I hoped our customers would be really soon. Next to them were stacks of cups and lids, and bouquets of straws. We had a little silver napkin dispenser on the rough wood front counter, and the dented cashbox right underneath it. There wasn't any cash in it yet. We'd put some in later this afternoon.

We pulled the pink-and-red checked curtain Tia had found in her aunt's linen cupboard across the front, like a door, and tied it shut with some ribbons I had knit. Then we picked.

"It's a lot easier picking raspberries, isn't it?" I said.

Tia nodded. "No backaches, and if they're ripe, they pop right off into your box. Do you know when we were at the store last week I saw raspberries for sale five dollars for this many?" She cupped her hand and cradled a small amount of berries. "So how come you guys can't make that kind of money on the farm?"

"We only get paid twenty cents a pound when the processors come through to get them. If we picked by hand and rushed them to the store, maybe we'd make more, but we can't do that. That's why the Quinns do their own processing. Papa can't do that anymore, and I don't think he wants to. He gets the machines in here and they get them out fast. But they crush them. That's why we have to sell them so cheap, for jam or juice."

Tia popped another berry into her mouth. "You sure know a lot for a city girl."

"I'm not a city girl," I said. But really, I was kind of both—city mouse and country mouse. It's just that I had no cousins. No fair!

"Tell me about your cousins in St. John's," I said.

"Many of them have lived here for a long time," Tia said, twisting berries off the canes and flipping them into her box. I ate one for every twenty I picked. A rhythm with a reward, that's what I say. And no dirty nails.

"They moved here many years ago because their dads found work, but a lot of them live together in smaller houses. Even though we had to wait, we got our own house, and that was nice. Anyway, we're a close family, so even though my abuela and some cousins are still back in Mexico, I am glad to be here with some of them."

"Do they work on the Island—your uncles, I mean?"

"Some of them do."

I spied a spider on her shoulder and flicked it off. There were a lot of spiders in the raspberry canes. She smiled her thanks.

"Some work in Hillsboro. They all come here to play soccer on Friday nights and some Sunday afternoons, though. We're very big into soccer."

We stacked our berry boxes one on top of the other and headed back to the shack. We mixed up a "test" smoothie. Divine.

"This is so good," Tia said. The foam coated her upper lip like pink shaving cream and made me giggle.

"I think so too," I said. It was good, like a chocolate-dipped raspberry but cold. I pointed to her lip. "You might want to lick that off. It looks like shaving cream."

"Don't tempt me," she said. "Just like my mother, I'm getting some hairs there that look like a mustache."

I giggled. "You're crazy. I don't see a mustache."

She rolled her eyes and nodded. "Yes, I have one. You'll see."

Just then Grammy drove up. She parked the car and got out. "Hey—ready to sell a smoothie?" We poured one for her, and she dropped a lot of change into our cashbox. Way more than the smoothie cost.

"Now you'll have change when the customers come."

Would the customers come? That was the question.

Grammy looked around the Pink Palace and smiled. "I knew you girls would come through. Just look at this place. Who would have thought of pink paint?"

"The most creative Tia," I said.

"Well, you girls can make a go of it. Real businesswomen, I know. What are these?" Grammy pointed to the sample cups.

"Mr. Quinn gave those to us. But how can we get anyone to sample them if they don't show up here?" Tia asked.

"We could take them somewhere," I said. I swatted a hornet away. It had smelled our sweet confection, too. "But where?"

"It's going to be a busy weekend," Grammy said. "Fourth of July."

"How about Reeder Beach?" Tia said. "Won't a lot of people go there?"

"Great idea!" I gave her a high five. "But how are we going to get them there?"

Grammy pointed to her fifteen-year-old Cadillac. "I'm not driving that boat for nothing," she said. "Mix up a batch tomorrow, and I'll drive you in. After I curl my hair, that is."

It just might work, I thought. It just might work.

A few more customers dribbled in that day. It gave us hope.

The next morning we got up really early. Tia and I made a batch of smoothies and poured them into the sample cups. We made extra and kept it in the ice chest.

Tia slid into the car first, and I slid a box of samples onto her lap. Her legs squeaked against the vinyl of the backseat. Grammy had a knit doily in the back window, along with a fake dog with a bobble head. The car smelled like spearmint gum and rose perfume.

Then I got in, and Grammy slid a box onto my lap. Grammy clipped the sunshades onto her glasses and drove really slow all the way to the beach. She had her cameo necklace on. So did I.

We walked out onto the beach and handed out samples and told people where we were located.

"Would you like to try a smoothie?" I asked. I'd noticed I was the talker and Tia was the hander-outer without us even deciding.

"Can I have another one?" A little girl ran up. "Can I have two or three?" She tugged at my back pocket.

"We'll stop over real soon." Lots of people said this! "Delicious!"

Tia looked at me, and I looked back, and we panicked. How could we stay here and give samples and also be back at the booth? Grammy wasn't going to hand out samples. She had a limit.

I took the box of samples into the store and gave one to Mark. "This is fabulous!" he said. He was unpacking roll mops and salmon and pickled squid. Thick nightcrawlers, like fat, chopped licorice ropes, writhed in their cans. Lots of fishermen would be coming to the Island, too. "Want to leave some samples on the counter?" Mark asked. "When anyone comes in, I'll point them in your direction."

I almost hugged him. Almost, but my senses slipped out of neutral and into gear just in time. "Thanks, Mark! We'll give you a free smoothie anytime."

He smiled, his stained teeth great motivation for two minutes with my electric toothbrush morning and night. "You can leave a sign in the front and some coupons on the counter, if you want, for when the samples run out," Mark said. "Can't have you set up here, you know. Regulations. You can leave a paper trail, though."

"Coupons!" I exclaimed. "What a great idea!" We set the box on the counter in his air-conditioned store and headed back to the Pink Palace. We spent the rest of the day whipping up smoothies—and coupons for fifty cents off, handmade since neither Tia nor Grammy had a computer. Tia biked the coupons back to the Minit Mart while I handled the slow stream of buyers.

From that very first day we had customers. First

just a few, then a few more. People told other people that our berries were fresh and good and tasted just like what people came to the Island to taste. By the end of the weekend we were making money. It wasn't at all a for sure thing—we'd still have to see what happened when the holiday weekend was over. But at least we had a little hope to cling to.

Tia's dad rode by on the tractor from time to time, checking on us. Tia waved wildly at him, and he smiled and waved his red bandanna at her. That alone made it all worthwhile. You could see the pride beaming from his face as he turned a dusty corner.

I crawled into bed at night tired but happy. My knees ached from standing all day, and my skin was stained up to the elbows. Tonight I really did deserve the title Strawberry Blonde. Or Raspberry Blonde, if there was such a thing.

Sleepy as I was, I made time to read the next few verses on Dad's plaque. I'd been sleeping with the plaque close to my bed, and I never took off my cameo necklace. Dad would be home really soon—a few weeks. My head swirled at the thought. I couldn't wait to show him the Pink Palace. I hoped there would be customers there when I did and that he'd be as excited as Tia's dad was. I prayed, "God, I want to hear from you. I'm listening." Then I opened my eyes and focused on the next two verses, John 15:6 and 7. *"If anyone does not remain in me, he is like a branch that is thrown away and withers; such branches* are picked up, thrown into the fire and burned. If you remain in me and my words remain in you, ask whatever you wish, and it will be given you."

I understood that. Papa had to chop out canes and dig out plants that didn't produce. They took nutrients away from those that did. Sometimes they were diseased and could infect the whole field. Was I remaining in God? Maybe now I was really growing. I prayed, sometimes even in the middle of the day, in my head and heart. I was reading these verses, and I didn't even have to pinch myself in church last week. No promises for next week, though.

"Ask whatever you wish, and it will be given you!"

Here's what I want, Lord. How do I grow closer to you? Hear you better? I'm not a faker, you know. If I'm going to call myself a Christian, I want to be a real one. A living one. One that produces fruit. And, also, if you have time, I know this isn't probably your number one priority, but it's mine. Where should I make my home?

The Christmas when I was ten I bought a book for Grammy called Grandmother Remembers. She filled out the whole book with memories about my dad and me and her and Papa. She hadn't mentioned Mr. Quinn, though! Anyway, one thing really surprised me. There was a question about regrets. Grammy was sorry that she hadn't spent more time running the farm. She'd always had a good business head as a girl, but when she'd told her dad she wanted to run the farm, he'd laughed at her *and said she'd best find someone to marry to do it for her. Grammy had written that she'd been so glad that she'd married Papa and had my dad, but that if she'd do it over again she'd be more of a business partner, too. She had a green thumb. She wanted the black fingernails to match. I was so shocked when I read that. She had a hard time convincing others to let her fit in new customs with old even as a girl. You just never know everything about a person, even about a person you know really well. Maybe that's why it was so important that we make it with the stand.*

CHAPTER EIGHT

Early every morning I put my "dogs," as Charlie had called them, on and ran. At the end of the run I thought about the fact that some people walk their dogs in the morning. I ran inside of mine. At that point I figured the runner's high was back and it was a good thing it was time to pick berries.

Tia met me in the field. She was already partway into her first box. Was she mad that she had to start without me? "How are they today?" I asked.

"Juicy and ripe." Her lips were red, and I pointed that out to her. "Breakfast," she joked. Not mad. Good!

I began to pick the berries from the lower level. Papa had said we could also have these eight rows of berries for our stand, but we still had to pick low as well as high. As I knelt, I saw the world from a new perspective. The morning wind caressed my face, drying the sweat. My skin was left with a faint salt residue clinging to my hairline. I had decided to pray each time I knelt throughout the day. *Dear God, please let us make some money on the smoothies. Especially for Daniel. But also for me and for Tia. And help me to hear you and love you and be a good example for you.*

Papa was in the barn. He came out. "Need an old man's help?"

"You're *not* old, Papa," I said. "I am so glad you're picking with us. Every summer we pick together and since we can't do strawberries together anymore . . ." Uh-oh. Better be quiet now.

". . . because I'm too old to bend down anymore," Papa finished for me. Oh no. He knew what I meant. He ruffled my hair. "It's okay, Nutmeg. It's true. But I can pick raspberries with you still." He winked.

Papa filled two boxes for us. It was just so cool how everyone was pitching in to help. He gave me a kiss on the forehead and ruffled Tia's hair before heading back to the barn and his experiments.

"Ready?" I asked as I stood up several full boxes later. Tia nodded. We hauled our boxes back to the cooler and let them sit inside while we both went home and showered and changed.

Grammy was gone when I left the house—off to a meeting for the Before the Bridge party. I made lunch—two lunches.

I got back to the Pink Palace just before Tia did. "Want an apron?" She held one out to me—it was pink and foamy like the smoothies. It was so pretty. I bet her mom made them. I took it and wrapped it around my waist.

"Here, I'll tie it for you." Tia tied it in back, and I felt it cinch in my waist.

"I like this," I teased. "It makes my waist look smaller. Do you think I could wear aprons all the time?"

She giggled and tied her own. "You can try, but you might get some funny looks. You look very pretty."

"Thanks," I said, blushing to match the apron. Getting a compliment from someone who doesn't give them easily was worth more. "I made lunch for us," I said, glad to have a gift to offer her, too. "We were getting kind of busy yesterday, and I thought if we could take our lunch break here it would be fun." She took the bag from me. Would she like tuna fish?

I mean, I hadn't thought of it before, but some people hate it. I wished I had made ham or turkey or something safe. Maybe even PB and J.

She put the bag into the cooler without looking. I guess I'd find out soon enough.

Within the first half hour we saw a car heading down the street. "A car!" I practically shouted.

Please, God, let them stop here, I prayed. *Please let them come and buy a few smoothies and then let more and more cars come in a long line, like a convoy or a traffic jam or something.*

"They're stopping!" Tia said. We looked at each other. It was Monday. It was not a holiday weekend. We had a customer. Yes!

A young mother got out of the car and opened the back door. Three kids tumbled out, one after another, like circus gymnasts. They ordered four smoothies. Tia whipped them up and I handed them over and then another car drove up. Pretty soon there were many people and a school of cars swimming up the road. We both ran the blenders and served. All of a sudden I heard my name called out so sharply I almost didn't recognize the voice.

"Meg!"

I whirled around and saw Tia standing there, hands on her aproned hips. "You need to take the money. These people have been waiting to pay. Hurry up!"

I felt the deep red flush through my face—and it

was no berry stain. The heat started inside and ran from my scalp to my toes. I mean, it's not like I was standing around watching the clouds puff by. I was helping her make the smoothies, too. I know she didn't like to take the money, but math was obviously not a problem for her, and she could have gotten over it long enough to help.

I didn't say anything right then. I tried to smile even though my angry tears were ready to burst onto the scene at any minute. People in line got quiet, too.

When things slowed down we took out the lunch and pretty much ate in silence.

"Thanks for the sandwich," she said.

"You're welcome. I didn't know if you liked tuna," I answered. I wasn't ignoring her, but I wasn't going to make any deep conversation, either. The creamy coolness of the tuna salad soothed my feelings a little.

"I do like tuna," she answered. "I'm glad you didn't bring peanut butter. Americans seem to love that, but it tastes funny to me." She held out a can of pop. "I brought one for you, too. I forgot to put them in the cooler, so we'll have to pour them over ice."

I drank the pop even though I would have rather been stubborn and said no, thank you. I was thirsty.

For the next couple of days we were still so busy that I kind of blew off the situation. Tia never said any more about it. I never asked because it was so unlike her. But still, it sat between us, like a little rock wall we had to talk around and pretend wasn't there and kept us apart. Our easy friendship was as over as strawberry season, which was sad, since the business was booming and I had really started to like her. I think she liked me, too.

Ever since the blowup we hadn't hung out at night. It wasn't so bad, really, because we probably did need a break from each other. I'd been reading a lot. And resisting the urge to spy on the Richards family from my upstairs window.

One day as we were packing up for the afternoon, Tia asked me, "Do you have a microwave?"

I nodded. "Grammy does. Why?"

"I want to try something my cousins told me about. I want you to help me. It's about this." She pointed to the very faint mustache above her lip. "Can I meet you at your house after dinner tonight?"

I softened. She had pried a couple of the rocks off the wall between us. "Sure," I answered. "Come on over." I loosened a couple of rocks myself.

After dinner Grammy and Papa were watching TV, and I went into the kitchen.

"I'm glad Tia's coming over," Grammy had said on her way to the family room. "I know you two get enough of each other at the stand every afternoon, but I'm glad to see you doing fun things together, too."

Tia came to the back door. "We need to warm this up." She handed me a packet. I read it. It was for facial waxing.

I smiled. "Has your cousin tried this?"

Tia nodded. "It worked, too. You can't take off lip hair with that dissolving foam stuff."

We turned the radio on and I grooved while I put the packet into the microwave. After just a minute or two we pulled it out and let it cool. Tia handed a Popsicle stick to me.

"You spread it on with this. You have to do it for me, 'cause I can't see as well as you can."

"Me? I thought my part in this was to heat the wax!"

She giggled and held out the stick. I took it, smeared it above her lip, and then she put these little strips of cloth across the top. Then she snuck into the bathroom.

I heard some ripping/zipping sounds, but no huge cry of pain. When she came out her upper lip was flaming red—but hairless.

"Did it hurt?" I whispered.

She nodded.

"Can I try it?" I asked.

She looked at my lip. "You don't have any hair there."

I held out my forearm and pointed. "I hate this hair. I look like an albino ape." Within minutes we were warming more wax.

I got the wax and the cloth on one arm, then went into the bathroom and ripped one two-inch strip off. I can't explain how bad that hurt. Imagine putting a bandage over a totally open wound, then ripping it off at full speed and pouring hot salt water over it. That might come close. Okay, maybe I exaggerate. But it hurt.

Tia came into the room and we both looked at my arm and laughed. I obviously couldn't leave it like that—with one stripe down the center of my forearm.

"You do it," I whispered. "Rip the rest off for me." She did, as well as doing the other arm, too, so it wouldn't look too weird. Well, more weird. It was already weird.

We sat on the porch for a while after that. "My arms hurt really bad when we did that!" I said. "It feels like one time when I was at the beach and hot sand blew onto my skin. It stung like needles."

"My lip felt like a hundred red ants attacking," she said. "But I wanted to see if it looked good on me. I have my cousin's *Quinceanera* to go to next month, and I don't want to have a mustache or a puffy red upper lip. I figured if I try it now, even if it's bad, I will have time to recover."

I rocked in my chair. She sat in Grammy's. I was okay with that, for now. "What's a Quinceanera?"

"It's a really big party families throw when a girl turns fifteen. It's like her 'womanhood' party. It's almost like a wedding. Everyone comes—all your relatives and every friend you care about. It's huge."

We sat there for a while. It kind of made me wonder if she would invite me to that party. Could she? And if she could, would she? Was I a friend she cared about?

"Any boys there you want to impress?" I asked. We hadn't talked about boys yet. It was kind of a new level in our friendship, and we seemed to be back on track after our fight.

"I don't have time for boys," she snorted.

"What about the mysterious Orlando?" I teased. She had brought him up once or twice before in casual conversation. She looked away and I knew I had struck gold. I didn't push her, though. I knew she was a private person and she'd tell me when she wanted to.

I ran up to my room and got a whole stack of my books I'd set aside and then ran back down. "Here, these are good ones." Tia was smart—smarter than I, probably, but she still needed help reading English if she was going to try to go to school here. Maybe. If she stayed, that is. I pushed the uncomfortable thought aside.

"Thanks!" I watched her as she walked home, to make sure she got there okay. Any friend would do that.

The next morning was church. Grammy looked at my arms a little, but by then the redness had died down so it was just smooth all the way. I loved it. Grammy said nothing so I sure didn't volunteer any info. That was one good thing about not having any parents there right now. Grammy wasn't sure what to call me on and what not to. I'd tell my mom. Eventually.

I was having a great day. The pastor was saying something that actually made sense to me. I don't know if that was because he was getting better or I was starting to tune in. Or both. Partway through the service, one of Grammy's friends snuck up behind us.

"Can Meg come and help in the nursery?" she whispered. Grammy nodded her head yes. I opened my eyes wide and looked straight back at her as if to say, "No way."

The woman looked at me. I shook my head no. She looked surprised but tiptoed away to find someone else. I felt Grammy stiffen in the pew beside me, so I pulled away a little, too. I sure wasn't going to get into the I'm-a-bad-baby-sitter-kids-hate-me deal with her now. But I also wasn't ready to be rejected by a batch of new kids and have the whole church see how lame I was with them. I wondered if saying no made me a bad branch. Unfruitful.

Grammy was kind of stiff for the rest of the service, but by the time we got home she was over it. Tia and I whipped up some smoothies in the afternoon, but we'd made a good amount of money and the business was established, so we closed by three o'clock. It was Sunday, after all. Weren't we supposed to have a day of rest? Maybe Mondays. I'd have to talk with Tia about that.

"Want to hang out?" I asked after we got the Palace tidied up.

"I can't. I've got somewhere to go." Normally she'd just out and tell me. Now what was happening? But she was mysteriously quiet on this. I wanted to ask, but I didn't.

Later on I thought I'd take an early evening run. I slipped on my dogs and ran down the road. As I did, I passed the elementary school. Several community soccer games were in full swing. I heard the cheering and clapping and calling out along with the dull thud of foot meeting ball. Hey! I thought I saw Tia there, on the field, and Pablo on the sidelines. Why not go and check it out?

I walked across the bumpy field, a few over-tall clumps of healthy grass here and there among balding patches of brown. As soon as I walked up to their field, it grew really quiet on the sidelines. All of the Spanish chatter died away and several people looked my way. Some of the women smiled little smiles, but no one said anything. I stood there kicking the dirt for a while. Then Mrs. Ramos saw me and came over to say hello. She was kind, of course, but seemed kind of strained. Like she didn't know what to do with me. Maybe she was mad about the waxing? I didn't know.

She offered a chair. It would be worse to just walk away now, so I sat down and watched. After a while people started talking again—in Spanish—and I kept watching, feeling weird and unbelonging. Tia came off of the field after the second half. Pablo had scampered to the playground with some of his friends. Probably as he saw me coming, I thought, feeling sorry for myself.

"Hello," Tia said. She seemed a bit awkward, too.

"Hi, I was just going to leave. I just wanted to drop by," I said.

"The game is over. I'll walk with you. We can go get a snack." As we walked past the clusters of her friends and family sweating and laughing and gulping water, Tia pointed to one boy. He looked at me and smiled, the first real smile I'd had since arriving at the soccer field. I smiled back, thankful for the gesture.

"He's the one having the operation," she whispered. "Daniel."

"I'm glad you're helping him," I said with sincerity.

We kept walking down the sidelines, toward the town. She pointed to a tall boy on the field playing defense. "Orlando." It was hard to tell from a distance, but he looked cute. She waved to him and he waved back.

"No time for boys, eh?" I teased her, more comfortable now that we were away from the crowd.

She smiled at me and said nothing. Sometimes good friends don't need to say anything. Were we good friends? Were we . . . best friends? I didn't know.

"No mustache," I told her. "It looks good."

"Has Charlie noticed your smooth arms?" she asked. I blushed. Zing! Payback. She'd noticed about Charlie and me. It's good to be understood.

We walked toward town, toward the little store at the entrance to the Island. It was bigger than Minit Mart, but I hardly ever went there. It smelled like old greasy chicken strips baking under orange heat lamps, made worse by the mid-July heat. We got a candy bar and some bubble gum and then started walking back. The night was gently falling, covering the town with a pixie dust of twilight. We chatted easily and decided to take the next day off, since it was Monday, and the real business came toward the end of the week. Plus, the next layer of berries needed to ripen. I hoped those eight rows would last us through the last couple of weeks of July.

"I feel at home here on Sauvie Island," Tia said, right before she and I parted ways. She was heading back to the soccer field.

"Me too," I replied. The truth was, it was home to both of us, to both of our families, and belonged to us equally, not two separate but one meshed way of life.

I didn't think of it then, but I did on the way home. Sauvie Island might *feel* like home for both of us, but it couldn't *be* home to both of us. If her dad

125

stayed, my dad wouldn't have a job. If my dad stayed, hers wouldn't. The Island was so small there were no other family farms that needed a supervisor, so her dad would have to move for sure. Most men ran their farms themselves. Most weren't as old as Papa.

I played soccer when I was younger. I liked it. Back then I always wanted to be an attack or a wing so I could score. So did most of the other girls on my team. I mean, scoring was why we were there, right? Coach was always hammering about how it was a team effort, that everyone was necessary, that goalie and defense were as important as anything else, if not more. We didn't listen, at least I didn't. I wondered—if I played soccer again, would I still want to be the center or an attack or a wing? Would I be willing to put the others up front instead and be a defender, lots of guts and pressure, no glory? I didn't know. I wish I could say, oh yeah, definitely. But I really didn't know.

CHAPTER NINE

W anna learn how to cook?"
Tia asked one day.

"Oh yeah, if you're up for a challenge," I
answered. We brought our pink aprons home
from the booth and met at her house.

She had spices and ingredients all over
the counter. The house smelled like a market.
Mrs. Ramos sat in the back room, knitting.
She was really nice to me again—no weird-
ness since the soccer game. I figured maybe

I'd just caught her off guard that day.

"We're going to make tamales!" Tia said. That afternoon I wrapped *masa*—corn meal—in a real corn husk. No kidding! I stuffed *machaca*—shredded beef—inside each one. I stuffed some into my mouth, too. Tia giggled as I wiped my chin.

In return, I taught her how to knit. I think it would be fair to say I would always be the better knitter and she the better cook, but by the end of the week I had her knitting little bookmarks. "Very nice. Tia never try before!" her mom said as she rocked back in a thick chair reading a big book. Her mom and I really were alike. I like big books, too. They don't end so fast. I don't like when things end. But something always has to end in order for something to begin. Which reminded me of something else.

"I want to make something really special for my dad's first night back. Will you help me?"

"Sure. Let me know what you want to cook and we'll make it together." It was a week before he was to arrive, but I still didn't know what I wanted to make. I wanted it to be kind of Islandy, but really special, too. *Lord, please help me find something that Dad will like and that I can make.* I hoped God had time for small requests.

On Monday we took the day off and biked to the beach and hung out. It was the third week of July, and we were on target to make nine hundred dollars by the end of July, which would put us right at eighteen hundred dollars by the third week of August—in one month—a hundred dollars more apiece than we had hoped for! One day off would be okay. I packed nail polish (the heat would help it dry) and a big towel and some sun lotion. I wanted some color to get through but wore sun-screen so I didn't fry. Tia, of course, was naturally browned and looked great already. "I almost wish your lip wasn't so smooth and hair free," I told her on the way there.

"Why?"

"You're so pretty already. You might give the rest of us a chance to compete." She rolled her eyes and passed me on her bike, and we finished the ride to the beach laughing and swapping secret hopes and fears.

"No samples today," I told Minit Mart Mark. "We're taking a day off."

"Nice," he said. "You need it." He tossed several pieces of blue-wrapped bubble gum our way. We each caught a few, and I stuck one in my mouth as we walked onto the beach. I took great pleasure in blowing a huge bubble. Grammy thought bubble blowing was unladylike.

We found a section of the beach that was warm, out of the wind, and not occupied. A miracle. "I brought red and pink," I said, waving the two bottles of polish in one hand. The sunlight filtered through them so they looked like rubies and pink diamonds sparkling in the beige sand. "Which do you want?"

"Red," Tia said. "How about you?"

"Pink," I said. "To match my complexion." We both laughed. I painted her nails and she painted mine.

"It always works out better if you help your friend and she helps you rather than each person doing whatever they need for themselves," she said, and I agreed.

"Here, I brought something for you." I pulled a book out of my backpack. "It's about two girls who live on an island in California for the summer. One girl is Caucasian and one is Hispanic, just like you and me. I thought you might like it."

Tia picked the book up and turned it over. "Thanks." She'd already read and returned the stack I gave her. Good thing Grammy believed in keeping lots of books.

"You always pick good books for me," Tia said.

"Like Gary does for me," I said. Actually, Gary and I had a lot in common, when I thought about it. I missed him. I'd make sure to talk with him when I called Mom next time.

We lay on the beach till lunchtime. "I'm hungry, are you?" Tia asked.

I nodded. "Let's walk up the road and get pizza." We walked up the street a little, past the signs that said, "U Pick Walnuts, 20 cents a pound" and "Fishing bait—buy yours here."

"Want some fishing bait?" I asked her.

"No, thanks. Sad as it is, I'm taking the week off from fishing," she said. We shared a smile. We both hate fishing!

We came to the same old Beach Pizza that we'd always had. We walked in and sat down and ate a slice. The offerings were small: cheese, pepperoni, sausage. Blah. Not like Gary's at all.

"We'd better make a plan," Tia said. "The raspberries are at their peak. They'll only last another week or two. We still have like four or five weeks of summer for our stand. What'll we do when the raspberries run out?"

I thought. "Well, we could ask Papa about some blueberry bushes. I don't know if he'll let us use them. We can get Grammy to chase him if he says no." We both laughed, then sat there, sharing our pizza and our silence in an old-friends kind of way.

We rode our bikes back to the Pink Palace and whipped up and delivered smoothies for Tia's dad, for Papa, and for Grammy.

"You girls are the nicest things," Grammy said, licking her lips. "I do think adding chocolate was the best idea I've ever heard of, Meggie." My heart swelled, and in her honor I slipped what was left of the bubble gum into the garbage, unchewed, on the way out to the field.

We walked together among the canes. Raspberry canes grow long and tall, and you have to bend them slowly so they grow the way you want them to. Papa had his workers all bend his into a shape that looked like a pretzel. I started thinking about Charlie, and then I kind of thought the canes looked more like hearts than pretzels. Canes grow on fences, and it makes them easy to pick. The whole point of being a fruit farmer is to have fruit, after all.

I spied Mr. Ramos in the field managing the workers, both English- and Spanish-speaking. He never let Papa do the hard stuff in the middle of the day when it was hot. He treated him as he would treat his own father. As my dad, who loves Papa as deeply as he loves me, would treat him.

We padded over to the blueberry bushes. The blueberries were as big as dimes and tight as a baby's fist. Soon the berries would be nickel size. They'd be round and blue and sweet with their little ruffled belly button in the center. They tasted good. But would they make good smoothies? I didn't think they'd be good with chocolate, and chocolate had been the big appeal this summer.

"Daniel was at church last week," Tia said. "You know, the boy who needs the operation. I know that he trusts God to bring him through. But I'd sure like his mother to be there."

"Me too," I said. "My dad will be home soon. I

understand about missing your parent." I hadn't called my mom for a while. All of a sudden I missed her, bad. Maybe I'd call her tonight.

Tia and I painted a second sign that said "Pink Palace: Island Smoothies—2 miles" and biked it down to Reeder Beach. "I'm putting it next to the one that talked about walnuts. After all, wouldn't you rather have a smoothie than a nut?" Tia nodded.

"I have a nut for a friend, though." I giggled and she did not. Uh-oh. Were we switching into hyper-sensitive drive again? I was ready to get huffy till I realized she probably didn't get it because it was an American joke. I explained to her that a "nut" also could be a silly person. *Then* she laughed. She was so good at American English almost all the time I sometimes forgot there were a few expressions she didn't know.

The sign was up. We found wooden stakes in the barn and painted them pink. Then we stuck them all along the roads from the sign at Reeder Beach and the sign at the Island entrance and called it a day.

I looked at my watch, which showed the time and date. Oh no! I looked at the date again. My dad would arrive in two days. "I need to figure out something to make for Dad's dinner!" I panicked.

"I'll come tomorrow night and help you," Tia said.

"Okay," I said and relaxed. Her cooking was always good. I think it was because she was such a science ace.

I turned in early, flipping through Grammy's cookbooks for good recipes, much to her delight and surprise. What would Dad like? Anything was better than army food. But he'd also traveled all over Europe. No way I could compete with that! I tried to think of something very homey. Very Islandy. Something Sauvie Island. I just didn't know what it would be.

Before I fell asleep I looked at his plaque and read the next verse, John 15:8. *"This is to my Father's glory, that you bear much fruit, showing yourselves to be my disciples."*

What kind of fruit should I bear, Lord? Blueberries? Lemons? I giggled. Time to call it a night.

"I love you, God." I don't think I'd ever said that before. Out loud.

~

The crowds at the stand were getting larger—and so was our stash of cash. "Well," I said as we cleaned up the Pink Palace the next afternoon, "it looks like we're on track to make the money we need. It'll be nine hundred dollars by the end of the month if nothing goes wrong. In fact, we could probably each spend a little and still make it."

Tia pushed the hair out of her eyes and smiled. "I'm so happy. It looks like Daniel's mom might be able to come. Who could ever have thought we'd be making money like this?"

I nodded and put my arm around her shoulder. "And I'll get my track shoes. Two pairs maybe—and the sports fees! You know, we really are a team. I could never have done this without you."

She smiled. "Me neither. Not that either of us ever *would* do it without the other. You know?"

The sound of those words rang tinny in my ears. Something was wrong. Maybe it was natural anxiety, or the fact that whenever something was going well in my life it often fell apart. Maybe it was a warning from God. I pushed the thought aside.

"I found a recipe for us to try for my dad, but we'll need blueberries," I said. "Let's go pick some and then head down to the store to get the few ingredients Grammy won't have so we can try it."

We walked over to the Sharpblue bluberry bushes—there were just a few—and found a few handfuls of ripe berries tucked here and there among the hard green ones. We picked some and I pulled my T-shirt out in front of me, improvising a little basket to carry them home in. They weren't as sweet as they would be later, but that was okay. That's what sugar was for.

We walked to the store to buy the ingredients for my special recipe, chatting about the summer parties coming up—Back to the Bridge for me and the Quince for Tia—and what we would wear. Tia liked strong bold colors, probably because she could wear them and not fade away. I liked pastels. Call me spring. Tia didn't mention my going to the Quince. After the soccer game fiasco, I didn't ask.

"I don't really have anything too good to wear," she said. "But of course, it's not all about me. It's about my cousin. So whatever I wear will be okay. My parents are saving up in case we have to go back to Mexico. They'll have Pablo's tuition to pay this year, too. Plus, we always send money to my abuela." I could imagine her in something beautiful and red, like her ruby fingernails.

"I don't know what I'm wearing, either," I said. "I pretty much always wear shorts and a T-shirt or jeans and a T-shirt. Maybe I'd like to wear something else. I'm not really keen on Grammy taking me shopping, though. Who knows *what* I'd end up with? I could ask my mom to send something else down. I kind of feel like wearing something more grown-up, you know? I mean, I'm a teenager now."

We got cream cheese and a lemon from the store and headed back to Grammy's. I cracked open the cookbook and stuck a big clunky spoon across it to keep the pages open.

"Here it is!" I pointed to the recipe. "Lemon Blueberry Cheesecake. Do you like the idea?" I watched her face. "Blueberries because it's on the Island. Lemons because my dad loves lemon. I prayed about it and God gave me this great idea."

Tia smiled. "Definitely. Totally special, and still a part of his home." She did understand.

We whipped up the ingredients. I tried really hard to not splatter anywhere, but I did get a few drops on the cookbook itself. "What's a water bath?" I asked. Tia shrugged. She didn't know, either. We looked it up in the back of the cookbook and then made one. You put the cheesecake pan, wrapped in foil, into another pan half full of water. It makes the cheesecake creamy. I licked the creamy tart-sweet spoon down to a tongue print on the bare polished silver. Who cares if there are raw eggs in the batter? Live dangerously. Yum.

When the cheesecake was done and the sauce made, we put it in the fridge to set. "When's he coming?" Tia asked.

"Tomorrow night, late. I don't think I'll be able to eat or sleep or anything."

"Okay. Dinner's soon; I'd better get going. See you in the morning."

I stayed to clean up a bit. Grammy would be in the kitchen soon to fix dinner. She was very hep on keeping everything perfect till Dad came home.

When it was done I grabbed the portable phone and took it outside. I wanted my mom today, somehow, even though I'd have my dad tomorrow. Maybe because of that. I mean, I wanted them both. At the same time. I always did, but I couldn't have that. I dialed home.

"Hello?" It was Gary.

"Hey, Gar," I said. "How are you?"

"I'm great, kiddo. A better question is, how are *you*? Getting ready for your dad's visit?"

"Yeah, I am." I changed the subject. I know Gary and my dad respected each other, but it felt ooky for me to talk about it. We chatted for a little bit about the neighborhood and the new baby. He was totally excited. He'd been working on the nursery.

"I painted your room, too," he said. "Really carefully. And I've got a couple of books I'll send down your way."

"Great! I want Mom to send some clothes. Maybe you can send them with the books. Is Mom home?"

"Nope. She's out shopping right now and I'm making pizza for when she gets home."

"Oh, you have no idea how much I miss your pizza," I said. "What are you putting on it?"

"Let's see. Goat cheese, sunflower seeds, shredded pepperoni, fresh mushrooms, grated garlic." I was drooling.

"Can you send a piece of that down, too?" I told him about my boring pizza lunch.

" 'Fraid you'll have to settle for the books, kiddo." I told him about my smoothie stand and how well we were doing. He was really proud. He said so, twice. Then we hung up, after Gary promised that Mom would call me later.

She did. I felt that heartache creep back. "The baby's moving. Here, let me put the phone by my tummy." I rolled my eyes. Of course, she couldn't see me.

"Hi, Baby," I called through the phone. "I—uh—can't wait to see you," I said lamely. Then I got all teary-eyed. I don't know why. I sniffled and Mom came back on the line.

We chatted about my dad's visit. "I'm going to send you another card soon," Mom said. "I'll put your clothes and the books Gary bought you with it."

A card. Good. I loved getting them from her. I told her I loved her—out loud, no knocking—and she told me back. Then we hung up.

I went into the kitchen. A splash of batter had splattered on the top cupboard. I got a chair and climbed onto it to clean it up. While I was doing that, I got up close to Grammy's clock. It had fruit on it instead of numbers—you know, a banana for a one, two oranges on top of each other for an eight. She sure did know how to work a theme.

At the bottom of the clock, I noticed a Bible verse in small print. Galatians 5:22–23a.

I went to my room and pulled out the Bible I hadn't opened since last Sunday. After finding Galatians I read the clock verse: *"But the fruit of the Spirit is love, joy, peace, patience, kindness, goodness, faithfulness, gentleness and self-control."*

I glanced at my nightstand, and saw the verse I had read last night. *"This is to my Father's glory, that you bear much fruit, showing yourselves to be my disciples."* I remembered my question to God. What kind of fruit should I bear? Now I knew.

I closed the Bible. *Thank you for answering me.* I was starting to hear from God. I knew for certain, maybe for the first time, that He also heard me.

Papa and I always walk among the raspberry canes early in the season when they are basically just sticks. Same with blueberry bushes. You stare at them, and they are sticks. Then, soon, it's like their skin breaks open in tiny holes, like pores, and blossoms begin. The blossoms are beautiful and smell good and attract both people and bees! Each blossom becomes a berry. The branch doesn't do anything. The main plant sets the fruit process in motion. And even then, the plant can't make the fruit. "Only God can make the fruit, my little Nutmeg," Papa tells me. The farmer's job is to keep the soil ready and watch for disease and feed the plant, but only God makes the fruit grow.

It does look like it might hurt, though, bearing fruit. I mean—it's growing out of the branch's skin, for goodness' sake. But what good is a cane with no fruit? I wondered if it hurts for people to allow themselves to bear fruit. Let's face it, what I was really wondering was if it was going to hurt for me to bear fruit, never mind anybody else. I had the feeling it would.

CHAPTER TEN

My dad flew in on a commercial flight—not a military one—so we could meet him at the airport. When we got there it was late and the airport was pretty empty. Probably because it was Wednesday. Most people flew on the weekends.

My heart felt like it was flashing like the sign announcing the plane's arrival. I hadn't seen my dad since Christmas. What was taking so long? I knew he'd have to go through customs, and then Papa explained that a bus would bring Dad from the international arrivals concourse to where we waited. *Finally* I saw the bus pull up.

You know, for old people, Grammy and Papa sure were smart. They hung back while Dad ran to me and I to him. I knew they missed him, too. I had only known my dad since I was born, of course, thirteen years, and they had known him for forty. But they waited. They'd really been paying attention to that kitchen clock. Clock watching. Ha! I looked down at the fruit of the spirit letters I had written on the sides of my running shoes, just to remind myself. I'd written the first letter of each word in between the stripes of my shoes. It was a code. No one knew except me and God. Patience. Gentleness. Kindness. Self-control.

Of course, my dad didn't exactly run, because he's a colonel, but he sure walked fast. I'm not a colonel. I ran. When my dad set his luggage on the ground and swept me up in his arms, I felt like nothing could go wrong ever again. He smelled like starched shirts and a little airplane sweat and men's cologne—not Papa's brand. He felt warm, like a towel just out of the dryer.

"Hi, sugar, I'm glad I'm home. It's so good to see you." He squeezed me in a bear hug, then pulled back and looked at me. "You're becoming a young lady."

I grinned. I was.

On our way out to the car, I had to stop myself from skipping. Skipping is not cool when you're thirteen.

"How's my best girl doing? How is the summer going? The berry booth?" Dad asked as we drove from Portland back to Sauvie Island. The trip would take only half an hour at this time of night.

I chattered on about the Pink Palace and Tia and our great gobs of money and how I had a surprise waiting for him in the refrigerator and I hoped he liked it. Then I took a breath. They all laughed.

We got home really late. Dad tucked me in that night and saw the plaque by my bed. "Well, look here," he said. "Wherever did you find this?"

"Under the bed," I said. "I can't believe it stayed there all those years—I mean, with Grammy being a clean freak, you know."

"I tucked it into my mattress pocket when I was a boy. I . . . I didn't want anyone to see it," Dad said. "And yet I couldn't throw it away."

"Why not?" I asked. "Why didn't you want anyone to see it?"

Dad pulled the covers up to my neck. "That's a story for another night. Maybe one night in your newly built tree house. Okay?"

Well, no, it wasn't okay. I wanted to hear about it now. But oh well. I guess I was going to have to wait; maybe we could talk about it over the special cheesecake tomorrow night. I slept deeply that night, with no dreams. The best kind of night.

The next morning Dad and I got up early to run.

I was glad I'd been running, because I could keep up with him. I told him about the Portland to Coast. "Charlie invited me to run," I told him. I tried really hard to hold my voice steady when I used Charlie's name, but good ol' Dad caught on anyway.

"So Charlie's grown up a little from the pesky boy, eh?"

"He's grown up. He's still pesky." I left it at that and so did Dad. Bless him. "I feel bad that I'm not going to run, but I will be in track next season. St. Helens has a track team, and so does my school in Seattle. No matter where I go to school I can run."

"I have to go to Fort Lewis after next week and talk with the powers that be about my future," Dad said. "They could retire me without question. They could offer to promote me to Washington, D.C. Either way, we'll have some choices, won't we? Living here—or not."

It kind of felt good that my dad was including me in the choices, but sometimes I longed for the good old days where adults just decided everything for me and I could either be glad or throw a fit. I glanced at the letters spelled out on my shoes. Okay, maybe not throw a fit.

After our run I went to pick berries, and Dad spent a lot of time with Grammy and Papa. He stopped by the stand for a minute, and in the afternoon we went to see what kind of materials we'd need for the fort.

Later that night, a few hours after supper, the grown-ups all sat down. It had been a hot day, but a cool breeze zipped through the window and door screens, and the birds sang outside. I knew the birds would pay me back for all those bird feeders. The setting was just right.

I opened the fridge and took out the glass plate. Everyone was waiting—in the dining room, not the kitchen. I straightened the white paper doily under the cheesecake and walked into the room.

"Here it is." My voice wobbled. Papa had set out Grammy's best china dessert plates, and Grammy had made coffee.

"Ah, cheesecake—that my daughter made herself." Dad's eyes grew moist. "My little girl is growing up. I don't want to miss it. And blueberries from the farm?" he asked.

I nodded. My eyes grew moist, too. Dad got it. Dad got *me*. Life was going to be okay.

≈

Friday afternoon, after Tia and I closed the stand

for the day, Dad and I went out to the barn to assemble some materials to fix up the tree fort. "Would it be okay with you if we invited Tia to help us?" I asked. After all, we'd been together when her dad had helped us fix up the Pink Palace.

"Of course!" Dad said. I left him in the barn while I went to get Tia. I giggled as I left him. Still the military man, Dad's blue jeans and shirt were crisply pressed—to work on a tree house! His fingernails were always totally clean and tidy.

I got to the Ramoses' house "Is Tia here?" I asked her mother.

"No, at her cousins'," her mom said. She smiled warmly toward me, and I was glad. I said good-bye and left. I'd forgotten Tia had said she'd be preparing for the Quince.

Day slipped into evening as Dad and I beat out the last rhythm of the hours with hammer and nail. I'd brought the leftover pink paint with me—for the inside. I didn't want the tree house to be obvious from the outside.

Dad and I sat up there and drank root beer from cold brown bottles just like we had when I was little. Sometimes, with my dad, I still felt little, but in a good way. He didn't bring up the plaque, so I didn't, either. Patience, I told myself, tracing the *P* on my shoe. He'd tell me soon enough. Or else I'd ask. You can only grow fruit so quickly, you know.

"Those shoes are falling apart," he said. "Maybe I

can take you shopping over the weekend. We can go to the Nike store in Portland. I can buy you some shoes."

"I'm going to buy my own shoes with the money from the Pink Palace," I said. I hoped Dad wouldn't be hurt. "It will feel like they really belong to me, then. Do you know what I mean?" I asked softly.

Dad smiled and ruffled my hair. "We each need to carve a place on our own," he said. "I do understand. How 'bout I buy an outfit for you and take you to tea at the Heathman and we'll just *look* at shoes?"

"Deal!" We did the pinkie shake I had taught him when I was a girl.

The next day I got up really early and met Tia. We tidied the Pink Palace, which was booming with business. I tied the curtains back just so with the knitted strings, and Tia lined up the few bottles we had left of chocolate syrup. I got the boxes flat. I arranged the berries in neat piles. I scrubbed down the freezer. Dad was coming that day to spend some time and "watch us operate," as he'd said. I told him to come right after lunch so that he'd see us when we were really busy.

He did. He stood aside and waited for a lull in the business. There were three or four cars in a row pulled to the side, with moms waiting and kids sneaking berries or playing tag in the field. Most days we were busy all day, but especially right after lunch when the moms and kids were heading back to Portland. Everyone loved the chocolate smoothies the best—we sold three of those for every plain one. It worried me a bit, and Tia, too. "What will we do when the raspberries are gone?" she whispered. I shrugged. I didn't know, either.

I saw Dad off to the side chatting with Mr. Ramos. Tia looked worried. I wanted to tell her that everything was going to be okay with her dad and with my dad and with how it all ended up, you know, about where we'd all live, but I wasn't about to make promises I couldn't keep. People had done that in my life and I ended up hurt.

Finally things quieted down and Dad came over. Tia mixed up a smoothie. "Delicious!" Dad said.

"It was Meg's idea to add the chocolate," she added generously. I smiled at her.

We showed him today's money in the cashbox. We deposited it in a safe at Grammy and Papa's house each night. "We've made a success out of this even though people said we couldn't."

"I didn't think they could," Mr. Ramos said as Tia handed her dad a smoothie.

"I made a big mess of it when I was a boy," Dad

said. "You girls have some real talent. Hey, Meggie, come here." He drew me aside. "Let's celebrate your great success—the hard work, the persistence, everything. Would you like to invite your friend to come with us to Portland tomorrow? I know you wanted her to help with the tree house and she couldn't."

"Tomorrow? I had thought maybe we could go on Monday when it's our day off. Tomorrow's Sunday, and we have a lot of customers on Sunday."

"Hmm," Dad said. "Tea at the Heathman is only on Sunday. And I've got some people to meet on Monday. Is there anyone that could cover for you for one day?"

Not Grammy and Papa. Too old. Mrs. Ramos couldn't speak good English. I looked at Tia, and beyond her, to the Richardses' house. "Maybe!" I said. "I'll be right back."

I ran to Charlie's house, and his mom let me in. "I'll get Charles," she said. He came downstairs.

"Hello, *Charles*," I said, giggling. But I quickly decided I'd better stop the teasing. I wanted him to do a favor for me.

"What's up?"

"I have a favor to ask. My dad wants to take me and Tia to Portland tomorrow. Would you and your brother run the Pink Palace for us? We'll get up really early and pick the berries, and we don't open till after church. It'll just be for like five hours. *Please?*"

I could see by the twinkle in his eye he was going

to say yes, but he made me squirm. He waited and waited. Finally he answered. "Okay. But only if our practice run is later that night, because you know Kiski. . . ."

"No bending the rules," I finished for him.

Later that night Charlie came over to my house and said he could do it. We offered to pay him. Of course he said yes to that, too. I ran as fast as I could to Tia's and invited her—and her parents said yes! I was hoping she wasn't mad that I had asked Charlie without asking her if it was okay—but I wanted to make sure the booth was covered before I invited her so she wouldn't be disappointed.

Our first outing, only a few hours away! I could hardly wait. We jumped up and down and I skipped home. Who cared who saw me? I looked down at my shoe. J for Joy. That didn't hurt at all.

Sunday morning at church was awesome. I felt God, really, like He was sitting right next to me, on the other side where Dad wasn't sitting. My dad has a really deep voice, and I love to sing next to him. We went home and changed and then Tia showed up. She had fifty dollars to spend. I know that was a great sacrifice for her parents. We'd make it last.

First we went to tea. The Heathman is *the* hotel in downtown Portland, as far as I am concerned. I mean, on my wedding night, I want to stay there. Not that I'm getting married for a long time or anything. At the front door they have a couple of dudes dressed up like those guys in front of Buckingham Palace—you know, all in red with tall hats on and stockings? Anyway, it was very official. The tea court is like a royal parlor.

"Wow!" Tia said when we walked in. I knew what she meant. A man in a tuxedo was playing a grand piano in the corner, and all of the waitresses—if that's what you call them—looked like princesses. No kidding! The furniture was like from a royal palace, blue and gold and very stuffy. I mean, not snobby, but because it had a lot of stuffing. We ate little teacakes and sandwiches with no crusts and tea. Lots of sugar for me. I'm not big on tea.

"Tia, tell me about your home in Mexico," Dad asked. He was always careful to include everyone in the conversation.

Tia looked nervous at first but then loosened up. Pretty soon she was chattering on in that pretty accent.

After tea we walked by the Nike store, and I saw just the shoes I wanted. They were $140 a pair. No kidding. Even if I had taken my dad up on his offer to buy me shoes, I would no way expect him to buy me shoes that cost that much. But I could buy them myself, soon, and run and run and still have money left over for warm-up suits and sports fees and everything else I'd need.

Next we went to Nordstrom Rack. "I think we can find something really cute for you in here," I told Tia.

"It doesn't cost so much money, but the things are nice." Tia had told me she hadn't been able to bring many of her clothes, and with money being tight, she didn't often get new ones.

We peeled through shirt after shirt and skirt after skirt on the racks of discounted materials. Tia held up an olive-green shirt. "No way," I said. It made her look yellow.

Finally she found a jean skirt she liked. It had a leather tie belt. Originally it had been one hundred dollars and was marked down to twenty-five. She held it up.

"Beautiful," I said.

We looked through the racks and I found a pink-and-yellow surfer shirt that went all the way to my hips—for modesty—but didn't look geeky. A washed-out jean skirt—not matching Tia's—finished it up. I found a pair of pink ice earrings and a pinkie ring to match.

Tia still needed a shirt. Finally, buried in the junior racks, I found one. Ruby red with a princess cut neck. I held it up and Tia smiled. Perfect. We found a pair of silver teardrop earrings to complete the outfit.

On the way home, as we talked about the coming week, I had the most fabulous idea. I don't know why I hadn't thought of it sooner! "Dad! Wouldn't it be great if Tia came to the Before the Bridge party with us?"

Dad, to my great surprise, said nothing. He shifted in the front seat a little. "I think you should talk about that with Grammy and Papa and also Tia's parents," he said. Why Grammy and Papa, I wondered. Wasn't *he* my parent?

Tia didn't look real comfortable, either. "Come on!" I told her. "You'll look great in your new outfit."

"I'd like to go," she said. "I'll ask my parents."

We got home soon thereafter. "Thank you, Mr. West. I had a great time." She clutched her Rack bag and ran home. Dad and I hauled our bags inside, too. Tia came back a few minutes later clutching a bag of books I had just loaned her.

"Wow, girl, you're reading where I'm at now," I said. "And in *two* languages." She smiled. I smiled. I could cook now, too. That's what friends are for.

I went back in and told Grammy and Papa how great the day had been and showed them what we'd bought.

"Charlie brought over some money," they said. I looked at it quickly. *What?* There was hardly anything there. Like, half of what we normally made. What had happened?

"They had a hard time, I think," Papa said. "I saw some cars drive up and then drive away because it was taking them so long."

"Okay, we'll deal with that later. But here's my important thought." I explained about wanting Tia to come to the party.

They looked uncomfortable, just like Dad had. "I don't know, Nutmeg," Papa said. "It doesn't always work so well for anyone when we start to mix too much. People like one another and consider them equals, but it might turn a party atmosphere into an uncomfortable one."

"One girl?" I asked.

"It's just that the rules for the party are that those who come are families who lived here before the bridge. Other families can come to other parties."

"My friends *are* my family," I insisted.

Papa softened.

"You're right, honey," Grammy said. "Just because it's never been done doesn't mean it can't be done."

I hugged her. I ran to Tia's house, but before I knocked I saw her in there talking with her mom and dad. They looked a little stressed. I guessed I'd better wait till tomorrow to see if she could come.

I walked back home and went running with my dad. I told him what Grammy and Papa had said about the party.

"I guess I'll have to wait for an answer," I said as we jogged down the road.

"Do you know why I like endurance running instead of sprints?" Dad asked.

"No."

"Because endurance is patience that is extended. If you wait, things normally turn out okay."

"You sound like Mom."

"Your mom is a wise lady."

Later that night when Dad tucked me in, I was knitting again.

"Baby blue, eh? What are you making?"

"I don't know. Maybe a baby blanket."

"Are you excited for the baby?" Dad asked. He didn't sound upset, but he did sound a little sad or quiet or something.

"Kind of," I said. *If it doesn't hate me,* I wanted to add but didn't.

"You have lots of yarn there," Dad said. "Maybe you can knit something for me when you're done." He kissed me on each eyelid, like always, and went downstairs to visit with Grammy and Papa.

Drinking all that tea today did two things: One, it made me have to visit the bathroom a lot. Two, it reminded me of one of the devotionals that Grammy left on her porch. Secretly, I liked devotionals, but I didn't want Grammy to know or else she'd think she won. Anyway, this one page said you never know what kind of tea is inside till you put it in hot water. Same with people. When things get tricky, you see what they're made of. I wondered what kind of tea I was. I kind of wanted to find out. I wasn't sure I wanted to get into hot water, though.

CHAPTER ELEVEN

I'd gone to the Before the Bridge party before. It was held the last week of July or the first week of August every year. I'd never gone as a teenager, though. Never with a good friend. Never cared whether Charlie would notice me or not. So this year really was different.

Grammy and Papa went over to the Grange Hall first to help get the stuff. It was going to be held at the Bybee Howell house grounds. The BH house is an old restored house on the Island, from when the first people settled there.

"Hey, Mom, did you know the original Bybees or Howells?" Dad joked. Grammy punched him on the arm. The Bybees and Howells had arrived like 150 years ago. It's easy to see where I get my sense of humor.

Dad got ready, too. White running shoes. Pressed blue jeans—with a crease. Do jeans even come, originally, with a crease? Does everyone in the military starch their jeans? These were questions that occurred to an ordinary thirteen-year-old who never used an iron.

I broke out my new jean skirt and the pink-and-yellow surfer shirt. I had a necklace of tiny pink and yellow beads and wore that, too. I hoped Dad wouldn't mind that I took the cameo necklace off for one night. After clipping my hair back in the little star clips, I dusted my face with powder that had a light sparkle to it and glossed my lips. I was ready.

Tia knocked at the door about fifteen minutes before we were to go. I could tell just by looking at her that she was nervous. Her parents hadn't been really happy that she was going, but they had finally agreed. Papa had told Tia's dad that he'd look out for her.

"You look great," I said, the screen door nearly knocking us both into the parlor as it swung shut. Her new skirt and shirt looked beautiful. "Something's wrong though," I said.

She looked alarmed. "Am I too fancy? Not fancy enough? Maybe I shouldn't go."

"No, no, you're fine," I said. "I just meant, with your hair that way I can't see the teardrop earrings too well."

I gulped and thought hard before I said what I said next. Charlie would be at this party, after all. It's not like she liked him, but there's no telling what *he* thought. Ah well. Chop chop. *I'm chopping the envy out, Lord.* "Would you like me to braid your hair? I could do a double French that would look really good."

"Yes," she said. "I'd like that." She sat down in the kitchen and let her hair tumble over the back of the chair. I ran upstairs and got two pony tail twisties; soon enough we were ready to go.

"My goodness, I'm escorting two lovely young ladies," Dad said with a grin. I rolled my eyes. I liked it, though.

We drove over to the party grounds. It was already pretty packed. The old guys manned the barbecues in the back, smoke filtering into the air like the native peoples' fires of old. I guess, in a way, this was the new native fire. After all, you were supposed to have lived here a long time to "get in." Papa was barbecuing chicken. He preferred beef, but Grammy preferred that he eat chicken. I had an idea he'd be

chowing a steak sometime during the evening.
Secretly.

We walked up to the soda and lemonade table. A
few people said hi to me, and I introduced them to
Tia. The women behind the table nodded politely,
but nobody really tried to make conversation with
her.

"Don't worry about it," I said. I knew what it was
like to be new and unknown.

She smiled. "I'm not worried."

We wandered around chatting with other people,
people I had known my whole life, practically.

"This is my friend Tia," I said to a woman who
always ran the Vacation Bible School program I'd
gone to when I was a kid.

"Hello, Tia, I'm so glad you're here," she said.
She seemed to mean it, too. If I ever overcame my
fear of children—unlikely—I'd volunteer at VBS just
because she was warm to my friend.

We toured the house together, which was great.
It did almost look like Grammy and Papa's house,
except that it was done up in old-fashioned furniture
and thick drapes the color of melted chocolate bars.
"I've never been in such a house," Tia whispered to
me. "I thought your Grammy and Papa's house was
fancy."

We talked about what it would be like to live
back then. "I'm glad I didn't," I said. "I wouldn't have
wanted to wear all those petticoats."

"They'd make your waist look smaller," Tia teased, reminding me of my apron comment.

Everyone there knew everyone else, of course, so I guess it might have seemed a little odd that Tia had come as my guest, because her family hadn't been here before the bridge. Whenever people did talk to us, they talked about memories and places and stuff she knew nothing about. I noticed she didn't eat much.

Finally, at the fireworks, we sat down with Charlie and some of the other kids from the Portland to Coast team. The sky sparkled like my lemonade. *Thank you, God, for no rain tonight.*

Charlie chatted with us for a while. "Sorry about the money for the booth," he said.

"Yeah, what happened?" I asked. "I'm glad you took over for us so we could go to Portland. But . . . I was just wondering."

"I don't know, it got to be too much for us. We couldn't make the smoothies that fast, and some of the berries got stuck, and there were rude people, and it was hard for Joey to make change." Joey was his younger brother.

He looked down.

I softened and said, "Thanks a lot. I appreciate all the help. We had a good time, and I couldn't have gone without you helping. It means a lot to me."

He looked up again. We didn't need to say more.

"Hi." Natalie sat right beside me. Finally! A

chance to get to know Natalie. I chatted her up about the Portland to Coast team and the high school track team and what she thought my chances would be if I stayed here and ran this year. "Is the team good?" I asked.

"Oh yeah, but there'd be room for you. Charlie says you're a good runner. If you weren't so busy running a business, you'd be on the team, too, eh?"

"Yeah," I said. "Maybe next year."

"What else would you like to know?" Her long brown hair was twisted back. I really should grow my hair out again. We talked about soccer and the whole school scene and where she was going to attend college. "Look me up whenever you want," Natalie said, "if you have questions about school next fall."

See, this was the kind of person I liked. She wasn't worried about if you "deserved" to be there or belonged. She just invited whom she wanted. Like I had with Tia.

Tia! I hadn't seen her in a while. Oh man, I'd been talking and then she'd been left out. I scanned the crowd.

I saw her; then, a minute later, I heard a little shout. I recognized the voice. It was Tia, and she was lying on the ground next to the lemonade stand!

I ran over to her along with Charlie and Natalie and the others in our group. The adults nearby, though, just stood there. I wanted to shout, "Help her!" but I knew that would make a scene, so I didn't.

I reached down to put my arm around her shoulders.

"Are you okay?" I asked. She nodded and tried to get up, but her foot looked all twisted. It almost made me sick to my stomach to look at how it was turned. She crumpled back down.

"I can't stand," she said. "I'm sorry." Tears of pain and embarrassment filled her eyes. I prayed, *Please, God, don't let her cry. For her sake.*

"Don't worry," I said. I saw my dad. He hurried over, looking worried, and scooped Tia up. We brought her to the parking lot and eased her into the car. Dad got a travel pillow from the trunk.

"What happened?" I asked, panic squeezing my throat.

"I tripped and fell. I'm sorry I embarrassed you," she said.

"Me? Don't worry about me," I said. *Worry about your dad,* I thought. I know I am. He's going to freak out. I shouldn't have stopped talking with her to talk with Natalie. If I hadn't been distracted, I could have walked with her.

"Shouldn't we call an ambulance?" I asked my dad.

He shook his head. "Too much money. She'll be okay."

Too much money? He must have read my expression. "I wouldn't mind paying, but her dad would feel bad. Let's drive over and see if they want us to take her to town to get it looked at."

My stomach felt like everything I had eaten all night had been thrown into our smoothie blender and whirled up. I hoped it would stay put. I didn't say that, though. I was more worried about Tia.

While I was getting Tia settled in the back with her foot on the pillow, the VBS leader and her husband came to help. "Thank you," I said. Actually, as I looked around, quite a few people had followed us, looking concerned. I felt better. Island people weren't all bad or all good. Like anyone else everywhere, I guess, they just took some time to get to know someone new. Dad got out of the car at Tia's, but we girls stayed put. I saw him knock on the door, and Mr. Ramos came to it. Mr. Ramos called into the house and he and his wife and Pablo came running.

Mrs. Ramos came close and peered into the car. She talked to Tia in Spanish. When Tia saw her mom she started to cry. We'd taken her shoe and sock off, and her ankle was swelling up pretty bad. Tia's new jean skirt was covered with dirt from the fall. I don't know why, in the middle of everything else, that made me want to cry the most. The outfit had held such promise and now everything was going bad.

Mr. Ramos looked mad. "We'd both like to go to the hospital with Tia. Can you stay with Pablo?" he asked.

Me? Baby-sit? I guessed so. What was I going to say at this point. No?

"Sure," I said.

"Take him over to Grammy and Papa's house if you want," Dad said. I was glad he brought it up. At least I could feed the kid licorice there. "You have my cell phone number."

They sped off toward Portland. Pablo and I walked into the house, where he burst into tears. I wanted to join him, but I couldn't.

One thing I noticed this summer. There were a lot more No Trespassing signs on the Island than there ever had been before. NO TRESPASSING! in English. Then, later down the road, NO ENTRA ILEGALMENTE in Spanish. Don't venture where you're not supposed to be. But weren't we all supposed to be together, old and new?

CHAPTER TWELVE

For the second time this summer I got a surprise gift. This one wasn't really a secret gift, but I didn't expect it, and it was just as sweet.

The week leading up to it was really hard.

"Are you sure you can do it?" Grammy asked. "With Tia having to be at home with her leg elevated for who knows how long?"

"I'm sure," I said. It wasn't true. I wasn't at all sure, but I wanted to give it a try, and I didn't want Grammy to shut the Pink Palace down. The raspberries were only going to hold for, at best, another week, so I might as well squeeze the last few cents out of the booth. Maybe there'd be enough for Daniel then. If Tia would take my share. Which she probably wouldn't.

"I'll help ya pick," Papa said. I didn't tell him no, because picking together and chatting was something we did every year.

"Okay." Truly, I was glad for the help, because now that the berries were getting old it was harder to find good ones. The old ones tasted moldy like two hours after you picked them. Gross. I wasn't selling science experiment smoothies.

I watched as Papa's smooth hands picked the berries. It's kind of weird that when people are young they have rough hands on the inside and smooth hands on the outside, and when they get old, like Papa, their hands are smooth on the inside, papery-dry, and wrinkly like a pug on the outside. Papa's hands and arms and even his scalp had spots all over them from being in the sun his whole life. "Have you been checked for skin cancer?" I demanded.

Papa laughed. "Yes, I have. But thank you for asking."

The sun was as hot as it was going to get now. It doesn't get extremely hot in Oregon, except in August. "I wish you and Grammy would put in air-conditioning," I said.

Papa laughed. "Too much money, Nutmeg. Wait till nighttime. God provides the air-conditioning if we wait for Him."

Waiting. Patience. I looked down at my shoe where the letter *P* was almost rubbed off. I'd better darken that one. I could write over the *J* for joy, too, since life seemed a little squeezed dry.

Papa went back to the barn then, and I went to the stand. Thankfully, there were still a lot of customers. When it was hot, the smoothies tasted better than ever. Mr. Quinn's ice guy kept bringing ice.

My feet throbbed from being up so early, standing all day making smoothies, and the constant heat. My sandal straps rubbed against my ankles, and I was getting a blister, I just knew it, which was going to thrash my running time.

"Hey, I've got to get back to Portland!" one woman said, impatiently balancing two toddlers while I mixed up smoothies for the customer ahead of her in line.

"I'm sorry, I'm going as fast as I can," I said. At that, the couple in line behind her left. I think it was the first customer I'd ever lost. I hoped it would be the last.

But it wasn't. The next day the line was long again, and I couldn't take the money and make change fast enough. There wasn't any shady area for the people to wait while I made the smoothies. Two people left that day and three the day after. The idea was to make this work *without* adults helping. I just hadn't counted on losing Tia for a few days.

Later on the third day, when I snuck a quick minute for lunch, I ducked under the counter top and let the tears streak down my dusty face for just a minute. I wanted to hide under there and let my jelly knees take a break and tell everyone to go home. Instead, I wiped my face with my napkin before standing up to smile at the waiting people. This time the customer was an Island person.

"Hey, Meggie!" It was one of Grammy's old lady game night friends. "How is business going?"

"Great," I squeaked out. Except that I'm losing customers who are running away faster than kids from a hornet hive.

"Where is your friend?" she asked.

"Tia?"

She nodded.

"She has to sit out for a while. Keep her leg elevated till the swelling goes down."

She nodded. "I'm sure sorry that happened." I looked her face over to see if she was faking. I have a good fake detector—you have to, in order to get through middle school as a girl. She seemed real.

"Well, thanks." I made sure her smoothie had extra chocolate in it. I figured I should probably start doing that anyway, to cover the fact that there were fewer berries and they were beginning to taste syrupy.

I finished at the booth early. Ran out of berries and closed it up. Later that afternoon I chowed a burger—no cheese, no bacon, but with sautéed hot peppers—and took a nap before running for a while.

I circled Tia's house a couple of times before deciding to stop. *Please let this go well, God. I'm kind of afraid her parents are going to be mad at me.* I was glad I had brushed my teeth after the peppers.

I hadn't been to Tia's since the accident. I took care of Pablo that night okay, but after they came to get him late that night, after the hospital, I thought I'd better give them some time to themselves. Tia was on medication, Grammy told me, for a day or two, and sleepy.

Mrs. Ramos opened the door. "Hello," she said. And she gave me a hug. I looked at her, fake detector in full swing. She was totally genuine. I hugged her back, pretty tight, I think, because she stood back and looked at me. I hadn't been able to hug my own mom through all of this, even though I'd talked to her almost every night this past week. I think I wanted a mom to hug me back.

I went into the living room, where Tia was on the couch, reading. The sound of mariachi music and the smell of frying pork leaked from the kitchen into the living room. I sat next to Tia. "How are you feeling?"

"Okay," she said. "I'm sorry about shutting the booth down."

"Hey, you're not supposed to be worrying about

that," I said. "And besides, I haven't shut it down."

She sat up and then winced as the pain from her ankle hit. "You're doing it alone?"

"Just till you can come back. Which will be soon, right?"

Tia looked at me. She didn't make up a story or make promises she couldn't keep, which I appreciated. "I don't know how long it will be till I can stand. Maybe two weeks. And even then—with crutches. The doctor said sometimes a bad sprain or a tiny fracture is worse than a break because there's nothing to put a cast on."

"I'll try to keep the booth up for another day or two. We're running out of raspberries anyway," I said. We talked for a little while and I handed a little sack of licorice to her. "For Pablo."

I stood up to go home. I knew her family would be eating dinner soon.

"Meg?" Tia asked. Her voice was different. Not guarded, like it had been almost always till now. I sat back down.

"Do you think we were wrong to go to the Before the Bridge party together? Is that why this happened? I mean, maybe I wasn't really supposed to go. Maybe mixing worlds isn't a good thing."

Tears welled up in her eyes. I remember one time when I pulled a muscle running. It hurt so bad that everything seemed much worse than it really did, because the pain from the injury colored everything in my world a little blue. I hugged her.

"We were not wrong. Really. You are my friend, and I wanted you there. I think some people have trouble mixing old and new. But we don't."

"People I know have trouble with that, too. Not me." Tia smiled.

"Lots of people were glad to see you there," I added. "In fact, one of them came by the booth today and asked about you."

"She did?"

"Yep. An old person, too. So don't worry about it."

She wiped her cheek with the back of her hand. "My new jean skirt ripped. Away from the seam, so my mom can't fix it."

"I'm sorry," I said. "There's no way to stitch it up?"

Tia shook her head. I understood. She wasn't one of those ripped and resewn punk or goth stylists. She'd never wear something like that. It was only clothes. But she didn't get many new clothes. And we'd bought it together.

Then she smiled. "I have something special to ask you. But first I have to talk with my dad." At that, Mr. Ramos walked into the house and smiled at me before heading to wash up for dinner.

"Should I come back tomorrow?" I asked. "I could bring some more books."

"Yes!"

"It will probably be early," I said, "because we're

running out of berries." I said good-bye to her mom, then went home. I hoped I could find something to bring tomorrow that she hadn't already read!

The next day I got out there early. Why not? It was cooler anyway. I slipped on a pair of cutoffs and a really nice T-shirt. I don't know why, but I did my hair. I was glad I did, because my surprise gift was waiting for me in the field.

He'd already picked two boxes of raspberries, which must have taken him a long time. Berries were getting scarce, and the commercial pickers had already been through.

"Charlie!" I said softly as I walked up to him. His arms were tan already, and muscular. He looked hot but not too sweaty. I hoped I wouldn't get sweaty. I also wished I had put some Love's Baby Soft on. "What are you doing here?"

"Research for the International Committee on Climate Change," he teased. "I'm picking raspberries for you. See?" He pointed to the flats. I smiled.

"Thank you so much. But aren't you supposed to be running?" I had seen the team jog by already, trying to take advantage of the early morning cool, too.

"I talked with Kiski," he said. "I can help out for a few days—maybe. If you want me to."

I grabbed a flat. Would Tia mind? Would she think Charlie was taking over? On the other hand, there really was no way I could keep up with everything on my own. Just seeing these flats of berries already picked made me feel hopeful. I looked down at my shoes and the *G* popped out. *Gentleness.* Trust me, it didn't come naturally. Only supernaturally.

"Thank you very much. I would really appreciate the help. It will be only a few days." After all, it was a sprain. Tia was going to the doctor today, Grammy had said.

We picked for another hour or so and got as many berries as we could. Whether or not Tia could stand up in a few days, the raspberries would hold out only so long.

We went back to the Pink Palace, and Charlie— while he didn't wear a pink frilly apron, of course— did a great job. I showed him how to use the equipment. "I'm sorry I hadn't shown this to you before we went to Portland," I said. He probably would have done a lot better if I had thought to train him and Joey.

"No problem," he said. He chatted with the customers and reassured them that Tia would be back. I took the money, of course, like always. We talked about school and running and music. It felt good to work side by side with him. We were a good team.

The runners jogged by again and he waved. "Everything okay?" I asked. He nodded but seemed distracted after that. We saw Tia drive out with her dad, Tia longwise in the backseat. When she saw Charlie at the stand, her eyes got wide and she connected with me.

I couldn't tell if she was surprised or mad. I just waved and tucked my hair behind my ear. I'd tell her later. Hopefully they wouldn't take her blood pressure at the doctor if she was stressing about this.

We closed the booth down, with almost all of the berries gone. "Take the rest home," I urged Charlie. I knew the pickers had already been through their field and they had no more berries. "Take this, too." I handed him a bottle of chocolate syrup, one of the few left. "Make a smoothie for Joey—on me."

"Okay." He twirled the bottle in his hand and tossed it back and forth. "See you tomorrow."

He walked home, and since his back was totally turned away from me, I watched till I couldn't see him anymore.

I hadn't seen Tia's dad's car yet, so I knew not to go over. I wondered what the surprise was that Tia had talked about last night. I stopped by the barn on the way to the house.

"Coming to dinner?" I asked Papa.

"Soon," he said. He and my dad were cleaning the barn. No, I'm not kidding. *Cleaning* the barn.

"What's going on?" I pointed to the neat stacks, the nearly empty corners. Nobody cleans their barns like this.

"The U of O is coming tomorrow. They like my hybrids and we're going to talk business." Papa's head flushed red again. "I hope they like everything."

"They're not coming to check out the barn, are

they? It's the berries they're after," I teased.

"I want them to see I'm a good, methodical person so they'll know my science is sound, too," Papa said. He sounded so, well, earnest right then. Almost like he was a schoolboy again. One time, long ago, he was. Just like Charlie Richards.

Dad winked at me. He seemed unsure of where stuff in the barn might be, and his shoes looked suspiciously clean for a farmer, but I could tell he was doing his best to help.

"Let me help, too," I said. I shinnied up to the rafters and tidied those up—Papa didn't use the ladders much anymore. We set all of the equipment in one end of the barn and made sure that the shelves were stacked neatly and all the paint and stuff was out of sight. Together we had it done in no time. Papa gave me a high five, and then Dad grabbed me for a hug. I walked into the house right between them, in a love sandwich. It felt really, really fine.

After dinner I grabbed a couple of books and headed to Tia's. When I got there, she was on the couch again.

"So what did the doctor say?" I asked.

She shook her head and frowned. "Have to stay off the ankle for another week. As long as it's propped up, though, I only have to stick on the couch for a couple more days. Then I can prop it up anywhere."

Oh. "Well, there really aren't any raspberries to

pick anymore anyway," I said. I was really sad that our booth was going to end so poorly but didn't say anything. I didn't want her to feel bad.

"Pablo! Bring it in!" she called in toward the kitchen.

I turned around as Pablo waltzed in wearing a small apron and carrying a frothy glass with a straw in it.

"Take a drink!" Tia commanded. So I did.

"Delicious!" I said, licking my lips. "It tastes almost exactly like—"

"Lemon Blueberry Cheesecake?" Tia jumped in. "What do you think?"

"Awesome! I mean, I don't know how you do it—keep coming up with great ideas."

"*We* do it," she said. "You chose the cheesecake recipe, after all, and knew it would be very Islandy. I just made it into a smoothie. The blueberries are ripe, and, well, I wanted to help some way, since I'm just sitting here with nothing to do."

"It's a great idea," I told her. I just didn't know how I was going to pick the berries and buy the smoothie stuff and all. I'd have to do it soon. Charlie would be able to help for only another day or so before he'd have to be back running on schedule.

"I wrote down all of the ingredients," she said. "And I'll be able to help real soon. I saw that Charlie stepped in to help out." There was a twinkle in her eye. "I'm sure that was very painful for both of you."

I punched her lightly on the arm. "Glad to see you haven't lost your sense of humor," I told her. I handed her a couple of the books I'd brought.

"I have some for you, too," she said. "We stopped at the library in St. John's today. My mom went in and got these for you." Hearing her name, Mrs. Ramos came into the room with piping hot tortillas slathered with butter. I folded one into quarters and took a bite. Delicious.

She stood there for a minute. "Thank you, that was so good," I said, thinking that maybe she was waiting for me to thank her.

"You're welcome," she said, but still she stood there. Tia handed a book to me.

All About Quinceaneras was the title.

"My cousin's is next week, you know, and I thought you might like to read up on it."

"Oh, I get it, so we can talk about it together and I'll understand," I said. That was really nice. Very thoughtful.

"No, so that when you go you'll know what to expect even if you don't understand a word of Spanish," Tia said, eyes twinkling again. "If you want to come, that is."

"You mean . . . me? Come to your cousin's Quince? As in, attend? As in, she wants me there, and you do, too?" I stood up and held the book to my chest.

"Yep. If it's okay with your dad, it's okay with

mine," Tia said. "We can plan what you can wear and everything. You won't feel, um, weird, will you?" she asked. "Because of the different cultural things. Old and new. Like we talked about. I mean, everyone might not be happy to see you there."

I remembered the silent soccer game. I remembered back to the awkward parts of the Before the Bridge party. What would happen *this* time? "Well, if you're happy that I'm there, and it's okay with your cousin, then that's okay with me."

"You gave me the courage, really," Tia said. "I wanted to ask you but was worried about what other people would think. Since you asked me to the Before the Bridge party, even if everyone wasn't comfortable, it helped me to be brave, too."

Mrs. Ramos, smiling, went back to the kitchen while we plotted and planned. My dad *had* to say yes. He just had to.

Later that night Dad came up to make sure my light was out. "Thanks, Dad," I whispered, not wanting to wake up Grammy and Papa, "for understanding about the Quince and saying I can go."

"Carve your path, Meggie, carve your own path," Dad answered softly. "Just make sure it's on His narrow road."

Outside of my Sauvie Island bedroom is a huge lilac bush, tree almost. It grows almost as high as the window. Every spring it has masses of purple blooms—more than any other bush I've seen at anyone else's house. The scent is thick enough to touch, almost, like perfumed mist. Whenever I smell lilac candles at a store in Seattle, I immediately think of the Island. One time I asked Grammy why that bush did so well when other people's didn't.

Lilacs aren't like other plants, she said. Other plants need constant care, need to be babied, and they whimper if the sun isn't just right or the water isn't just right. Lilacs actually do better when times are hard. No sun? It's okay. We'll make blooms anyway. Little water? Watch us go. They're tough little plants, determined to make it work where other plants give up.

I like lilacs.

CHAPTER THIRTEEN

The morning of the Quince was a mix of sorrow and joy. Joy, obviously, because a terrific party was happening that night. I was going with my great friend and we were both wearing groovy dresses and *Natalie* had loaned me some strappy lavender sandals. How cool was that? The sadness was because Dad was driving up to Fort Lewis that day. There was a little spread of worry there, too, like frosting between those two layers. Would I be left out at the Quince? And when my dad came back in a couple of weeks, his decision, no matter what it was, would change both of our lives. Tia's, too.

"My ankle hurts," I told Dad after we'd been running for about three miles.

"It's the shoes. You need new shoes. The support on those is shot. You shouldn't wear running shoes more than two or three months at the most. You sure you don't want me to leave some cash before I go?"

I shook my head. "Nope. I'm buying some when we divvy up the money at the end of the summer. It's important for me to see the whole amount at once. Like a trophy."

He reached over and patted my shoulders, and my T-shirt stuck to my skin. I breathed in the one-month-per-year humidity. I could tell by Dad's smile that he was proud of me. "You're doing so well. How are the blueberry cheesecake smoothies selling, businesswoman?"

"Great," I said. "And Tia's coming back to work at the booth, so that will be even better. Not that Charlie isn't doing a good job," I hurried to add. "But he's got his race to run. He was supposed to quit helping last week, but then Tia couldn't get off the couch. I guess he worked it out with Kiski somehow."

"I suspect you rather enjoy your time at the booth with Charlie," Dad said. "What do you guys talk about?" I felt the protective Daddy Bear in him.

"We talk about school, you know. He's going to high school next year," I said. "I think he's excited to be going to St. Helens. And running. The Portland to Coast next week, you know. Can we change the subject now? Like, when will you be back?"

"In a week or two. I'll go up to the post and talk with my commanding officer and see what lies ahead. I will either retire as a lieutenant colonel and stay here and run the farm, or I'll be promoted to full bird colonel and live in Washington, D.C. Then I'd travel more and be a liaison to other nations for the army."

"Will you have a choice?" I asked.

"Maybe," Dad said. "They might just retire me. Or they may give me a choice. I'll let you know when I know. It's not something they'd talk about over the phone."

Which meant he wouldn't talk about it on the phone, either. It'd have to wait till he got home. Home to Sauvie Island, I wanted to add, but didn't.

After a breakfast of blueberry cheesecake pancakes with lemon sauce (I knew how to work a theme, like Grammy), Dad took off and I headed to the Pink Palace. Charlie had picked some berries already and Tia met us out there.

"I can hobble now," she said. "But I can't stand for very long. Doctor says maybe fifteen minutes out of every hour, tops. Then I have to prop it again."

"Sounds good."

Charlie stood in the back of the booth. He didn't seem to know what to do.

"So, all ready for tonight?" Tia asked. "I've got my dress ready and all that. I'm going to the church service with my family and then we'll meet you there. Orlando is my escort," she said shyly.

Charlie came to life. "Who is your escort, Meg?" He tried to sound cool. His face was red, though, like Papa's scalp when he tried too hard.

"I don't need an escort," I said. "I'm just a guest, not a member of the court of honor. I'll just sit with Tia's family." I knew almost everything there was to know about the Quince now. From the book, of course. I didn't want to embarrass Tia tonight.

"Oh yeah, right," he said, and smiled. "I guess you guys don't need me today. I'll leave you to your chick chat and go do my run."

Tia threw a blueberry at him and I did, too. He ran away, back toward his house. I wanted to call out thanks for getting up early and picking the blueberries today, but he was already out of earshot. It kind of squeezed my heart. I hoped I didn't joke so much that people didn't know how I really felt.

"Well, do you think we can rearrange things so that you can do the smoothie blending down here?" I asked. I looked at the wooden crate that we'd tipped over to use as a table for the cashbox. Would the cord to the huge blender reach? Could I bring the berries and cream cheese and ice to her without tripping?

"I can do the money," Tia said softly. "I think that might be easier since I can't stand too long."

I sat down next to her, thankful for once that there were no customers. Birds chirped quietly outside of the Pink Palace, and the scent of Grammy's rose gardens washed over the morning dew. "You want to do the money? Like, take the money and make change and everything?"

She nodded. "There was a reason I didn't want to do it before. One time I was in charge of the money at the carnival at our school. We were raising money and there were lots of booths—pop-a-balloon booths and game booths and places to buy candy and treats. I sold tickets and kept the money. There got to be quite a crowd sometimes, and during one of those times, someone must have snuck up when I wasn't looking and stole almost all the money. At first everyone thought I had stolen the money. Nobody would talk with me at school. I found a note in my school bag that said, *'¡Ladron!'* Thief. I told them someone else had stolen the money, but not everyone believed me. The next year they asked someone else to do the money. They said I could make cakes to sell if I wanted to. I didn't."

I put my arm around her shoulder. "I would never think you were a thief. Even if every dollar was gone. You're the kind of person who gives and doesn't take."

I saw tears well in her eyes, spill over a fence of thick black lashes, and trail down her smooth brown cheeks.

"Thank you," she said. "If it were my Quinceanera tonight, you'd be a *dama,* one of my maids of honor."

It's amazing how fast someone can become important to you. We made smoothies and talked and shared secrets all afternoon. One secret I didn't tell her—what I had planned for her for the last week of summer.

That afternoon, business slowed down around three o'clock, so we closed up the Pink Palace for the day. Tia left to get ready at her house. Papa said he'd drive me over so Mr. Ramos didn't have to leave St. John's to come and get me. I think Papa wanted to check out where I'd be, too. Papa Bear again.

"I never thought I'd say this, but can I borrow your rollers?" I asked Grammy. She giggled—Grammy could giggle!—and got them out of her bathroom. "Let me roll them up for you," she said. "Then I think you should call your mom while your hair sets."

That was one good thing about Grammy. Even when I lived there all summer, she never tried to pretend that *she* was my mom instead. I think she would have liked having a daughter. I think she'd hoped that was what my mom would be, and it didn't work out.

"How did the smoothies sell today?" Grammy asked as she rolled one pink-toothed roller after another into my hair.

"Fabulous," I said. "We are totally going to make our goal."

Grammy stopped rolling for a minute. "Did I push you too hard?" she asked. "Did you want to do the booth or did you do it because I pushed? I know I can be pushy. I try not to be."

I sat there and thought. She knew I'd be honest. I wasn't going to change now. "I didn't want to do it at first because I thought Tia was snobby and it just didn't seem like it would work. I think we both did it because we didn't want to let you down. But now we're really glad to be doing it together. It made me so excited about running my own business when I grow up. Tia wants to be a scientist. I want to run a business."

Grammy smiled and finished the last roll.

I looked in the mirror. The rolls were really tight. If she wanted to, she could roll sushi!

I went and called my mom.

"Hey, I'm getting ready to go," I said.

"Me too," she answered.

"What do you mean?" I asked, panic filling my throat.

"I'm having mild contractions. It'll be any time

now. Hours or days. Or even a week. You just can't tell for sure."

The baby!

"Call me," I said. "I love you, Mom. Nothing will go wrong, will it?"

"Nope. It always works out okay. Remember?"

I smiled. "You're right. I will pray for you. For Gary. For the baby." For me, I wanted to add, but didn't.

"So—tell me about the Quince," Mom said.

I took the phone into my bedroom and closed the door. "Okay, this is what I've learned," I said. I opened the book and looked through the pictures, filling her in.

"See, this is like a growing-up ceremony for girls when they turn fifteen. It's, like, from childhood into adulthood. Isn't that cool?" I twirled a loose strand of hair around my fingers.

"The girl is all dressed up really fancy. She wears a tiara on her head—that is to show her success at crossing from childhood to adulthood. She gets a new pair of earrings from her mom and dad. The earrings help her to remember that she should always listen to God and pay attention to whatever is happening around her. She gets a beautiful doll. The doll is like the last little piece of being a girl. All over the doll are these cool satin ribbons with her name on it. During the night she goes all through the crowd and unpins one ribbon from the doll for each guest. Isn't that awesome?"

The rollers were starting to bite into my head. How long did they have to stay in?

"I'm sure it will be a lovely evening," my mom said. "We'll have a party for your sweet sixteen birthday, too—wherever you live. Although I don't know if you'll get a tiara."

"Really? Thanks! And, ah, no tiara would be great."

"You'd better get going. Did you get my package?"

"Yes, thanks! I'm so glad you sent that lavender dress. I was going to wear it for church, but I'm wearing it tonight. I didn't really have anything dressy, so this worked out great."

"Was anything else in the box?" Mom seemed intense.

"Yeees . . ." I said. "The books from Gary. They look great. I'll dive into one tomorrow. He always knows just what to buy. It's eerie. I suppose he's buying *Pat the Bunny* now, too, for the baby?"

Mom laughed. "Yes, he is. Did you see the card?"

"No. No card. Where was it?"

"In the box, I think," Mom said. "But listen—look for it when you get home. Don't open it now. It's something to read when you're not in a rush. Okay? Then give me a call about it after your dad comes back from Fort Lewis. Has he left?"

"Yes, he left this morning. Is everything okay?"

"It's just fine," Mom said. "Call me tomorrow after the Quince and tell me all about it, okay? Love you." She knocked on the phone three times.

I knocked four times back and hung up. I looked at the clock. Wow! Forty-five minutes and I'd have to go!

I couldn't stand the curiosity, though. I ran down to the barn, where we kept the recycling and garbage before it was picked up. I found the cardboard box. Stuck in the bottom of the box was the card.

I carried it upstairs, tempted to open it right then. *Patience,* I remembered from the fruit of the Spirit clock. My mom asked me to wait. *Self-control.* I set the card aside to read when I got home later.

Papa met me downstairs at the door. Even though he wasn't going to the party, he'd put on a tie to drive me.

"You look very handsome, Papa," I said.

"I couldn't escort my best girl with dirty jeans and boots, now, could I?"

We got into the old Cadillac, me in the front for once, almost swallowed up by the smooth leather in the huge seat. Papa gunned the engine and we set off. "Are you worried?" Papa asked.

"Nope. Tia will be there, and her family. They'll watch over me."

"Call if you want me to pick you up. And don't break your leg," Papa joked.

I laughed with him. "One injury is enough. Tia's got that covered."

He pulled up to the rented hall. They'd had a church service earlier, just for close family, but by the look of the parking lot everyone had made it over here already. Papa dropped me off in front and let the car idle. I think I was the only blond person in sight. Spanish chattering filled the air around me, but of course I couldn't understand a word of it. I tugged on the strap of the lavender dress and walked toward the door. Just like at the soccer game, people stopped talking as I walked by. There were a few warm smiles, for which I was thankful. A few hard stares, too.

Suddenly Pablo ran out the door and down the steps. "Licorice?" he asked. I opened my little silk purse and took out a small bag, so glad I had thought to bring some. I handed it over and he smiled and grabbed my hand. The crowd around me let Pablo and me pass into the hall. Papa waved and drove away. I wished he had come inside instead.

Tia had told me there would be a mariachi band. I saw them playing now, all dressed in black with their wide-brimmed, embroidered fringed hats bobbing up and down with the trumpet beat. I could smell the food steaming in silver chafing dishes in the back of the room. Pablo took me to the table where his mom and dad and Tia sat.

Since the girls in the honor court were all dressed similarly, I noticed that Tia wasn't sitting with them.

"Hey!" I said.

"I'm glad you're here," she said. "And you look so pretty! Here"—she pinned a little white rose on my dress—"there were extra so I took one for you."

It looked nice. It smelled good, too.

"Why aren't you sitting with them?" I nodded toward the other damas surrounding Felicia, Tia's cousin, the Quince.

"My official duties were over after the church service because of my ankle. I wanted to sit here with my family for the party," she said. And with me, I knew she meant. I noticed that Orlando was at our table, too. There were fourteen people who attended the Quince, and so the star of the day made number fifteen. Tia was the only member of the court of honor not sitting up front. A few people sniffed toward me.

The tables were all done up in rose tablecloths, and in the center of each table was a doll made of—clay? "What's that?" I asked Tia.

"A *Migajon* doll," Tia explained. "Just like the Quince has a beautiful ceramic doll with all of her ribbons on it, the Migajon reminds us of times when we couldn't afford ceramic dolls and the women in the family made them from bread dough."

"Cool!" I said.

Tia took my hand and hobbled over to the guest book. It was a beautiful album all done up with ivory roses. The pen had a long feather attached to it. I knew just then what I wanted to write.

"May you always plant seeds of love, joy, peace, patience, kindness, goodness, faithfulness, gentleness, and self-control in the lives of those around you. Galatians 5:22–23. Thank you for inviting me. Sincerely, Meg West."

"Do you want to go and say hello to Felicia?" Tia asked.

"Sure. By the way, you look great." Tia's light blue dress coordinated with the rest of the court of honor. Honestly, light blue wasn't her best color, but her mom had pulled her hair back in light blue combs, too, and that made it look really special. All the honor court girls wore light blue.

Felicia was sitting at the center table with her mom and dad. Her hair cascaded over her shoulders; her rose dress had lacy sleeves that went all the way to her wrists and it had a sweetheart cut at the neck. She looked beautiful. Tia introduced us in Spanish.

"Nice to meet you," I said to Felicia. "Thank you for inviting me."

"Thanks for coming," Felicia said. Her English was perfect. I wondered why the Spanish introduction?

"Thanks for being such a good friend to my cousin, too," she continued. "I know she was worried about moving over here. We hope she can stay."

"She's a great friend for me, too," I said. We left

then, as there was a huge crowd of people waiting to talk with Felicia.

"Why did you introduce me in Spanish?" I asked.

"For her mom and dad," Tia said. "Did you see that gorgeous ring on her finger?"

"She's not engaged, is she?" I asked, horrified.

"No! The ring is from her mom and dad and is to show her responsibility to her family, her community, and to God. She got a new Bible, too."

"Very cool," I said. "What does the food symbolize?"

Tia laughed with me. "Hunger! I need to sit down. But you can go up to the buffet with my parents and Pablo."

We went back to the table. "Do you want me to get a plate for you?" I asked. "You must be starved."

Orlando blushed and spoke up. "I, ah, think that's my responsibility, as escort, of course," he said.

I winked at Tia. "Of course."

I loaded up on hot rice and chicken mole and hand-rolled tamales. The tender chicken broke apart on my tongue, and the creamy mole sauce was like a bitter, spicy chocolate. Delicious! The lemonade fizz of the punch tickled my nose but made a perfect foil for the spicy food. The chatter still stopped whenever I passed by, but usually only for a minute, and I heard "Tia" whispered wherever I passed. People must have been saying she brought me. Orlando spoke great English, as did most of the people Tia's age, so I had plenty of people to chat with. A couple of people looked disapproving and remained silent.

"Hello," I said to one lady as we waited in line for the bathroom. She stared at me for a minute and then turned away without answering. I heard her say, "Tia," too.

After an hour or so the cake was cut. This time Orlando brought back a piece for both of us. The band struck up again. Mr. and Mrs. Ramos danced, but I mostly stayed with Tia.

"Do you think you can dance once?" Orlando asked Tia, in English—for my benefit, I guess.

"I think so," she said, trying her best not to hobble onto the dance floor.

Pablo grabbed my hand. "Me too!" We went out and danced one dance to the mariachi band and giggled and twirled together, then made sure to sit down before Felicia brought around the ribbons and thanked her guests. I slipped mine into my satin purse. Some of Tia's other cousins came around and talked with us into the night. They were so fun!

"Please come to my Quince," Tia's cousin Sara said to me on her way out. "It will be next December."

"Oh yes, please come," Sara's mother said and gave me a tight hug. I noticed that Daniel was there, too, the boy Tia was going to give her smoothie money to. He looked uncomfortable. His dad was nearby, but this was definitely a woman-run event.

Daniel's mom was still in Mexico.

It had been a night to remember, and I tried my best not to fall asleep in the car on the way home.

Grammy was knitting in the parlor, waiting for me to arrive.

"Did you have a nice time?" she asked as she kissed me good-night.

"I really did. I'll tell you about it tomorrow," I said through a warm yawn. I trudged upstairs and saw the card from Mom—almost forgotten—on my dresser.

I stuck my finger under the corner and slit open the envelope, then pulled out the card. It had a pair of knitting needles stuck into a ball of yarn on the front of it.

"We're quite a pair!" it said. I opened it up. "That their hearts might be comforted, being knit together in love . . . Colossians 2:2a," was printed inside.

"Dear Meg," Mom wrote on the inside cover of the card. "I wanted to let you have some time to think about your decision this summer, where you should live for the next couple of years. The summer is coming to a close, and you must make the choice that seems best to you, in prayer, with my blessing. No matter where you live, where you travel, or where you go, my heart will always be knit together with yours. Nothing can change that. Let me know what you decide so we can plan for school, soon. I love you. Mom."

I sat by the window, looking out over the fields I loved so much. I hoped it wasn't totally dumb to write that Galatians verse in Felicia's guest book and that she didn't think I was trying to be Miss Holy Roller. I guess it's just that I'd been thinking about it. Even though I don't like science like Tia does, I do remember being totally interested in seeds, even as a little girl. I loved the mix that came in a bag and you didn't know what it was till you scattered and grew them.

Even then, I know that a lilac tree scatters only lilac seeds. It can't grow anything else. Strawberries can only scatter seeds that are inside them—strawberries. They couldn't try to fake it and grow, say, blueberries if they wanted to. What was inside me? What would I scatter? What would I grow?

CHAPTER FOURTEEN

I called my mom the next day and told her all about the Quince. We didn't talk about my decision, of course, because Dad wasn't back yet. I did tell her, "I got the card."

"Okay," she said.

And that was it. I think she was distracted, anyway, because she kept having contractions. But the baby wasn't coming. The doctor said if it didn't come in a few more days, they would induce her. Otherwise the baby might be stressed. That stressed us all.

That whole week Charlie came out to help us pick blueberries in the morning. It was awesome, because even though Tia's ankle was getting better every day, it still hurt when she stood too much. This last morning, though, she was doing great. But we'd decided to close the booth down anyway. We'd planned to stop before the very end of summer so we could do a few other things, too.

"Thanks for helping us with the berries," Tia told Charlie. "But you'd better go and get ready for the Hood to Coast race, I mean, Portland to Coast. We're going to come and watch and cheer you on tomorrow morning. Some of my family and friends are even coming from St. John's. It's one reason why we've closed the booth today instead of tomorrow. You guys will run by here in the late morning, right?"

"Ah, right," Charlie said. "I guess everyone is meeting at the bridge and then driving over to the highway to cheer the team on as they jog by. So I'll see you guys there?" He looked at me.

"I wouldn't miss it," I said. Charlie smiled, tugged his baseball cap lower over his head, and jogged off to his house. I hadn't seen the team run by for a couple of days. Charlie said they'd been practicing off the Island, where there were more hills.

Grammy had told everyone, and I mean everyone, that this was the last day for the smoothies.

Mark had handed out "Buy one, get one free" coupons at the Minit Mart, and it seemed like everyone on the Island was there. Good thing Charlie had helped with the berries one last day!

"I'm glad to see your smoothie business is doing well, young lady," Mr. Quinn told me as he ordered his smoothie—no lemon. "Living near your Grammy is bitter enough," he teased. He turned toward Tia. "Your leg is better? There have been quite a few of us praying for you since the accident."

"Really? I mean, oh, thank you," Tia said. She looked at me and raised her eyebrows.

The woman in line after Mr. Quinn must have overheard. "Yes, and I'd like to make sure you come to the Before the Bridge party next summer, too. That wasn't a very nice introduction to it. We'll make sure to pull the loose roots. Promise!"

I scooped extra blueberries into her smoothie. Tia gave her one of our "special customer only" napkins when she handed back the change. Those napkins had crinkle-cut edges and were much prettier than the plain ones. Mr. Quinn got one, too. After all, he'd set us up with the ice man!

Later that afternoon the crowds melted away into the afternoon sun, leaving only a puddle of past experiences and the sweet scent of the berries. Tia took the curtains down. Papa took the blender and ice chest back for us. I scrubbed the wooden counters, but some berry stains stubbornly remained. I liked it better that way. I didn't want to scrub my memories clean. We brought the table and chairs into the barn. The cashbox, too.

We sat together on the barn floor, eating a late afternoon tuna sandwich, and counted the money. We knew how much we'd deposited into the bank last month, minus expenses we'd paid out for ice, syrup, yogurt, and paper products. I dumped this month's earnings out of the safe, and we divided it between us. There were stacks of money.

"Including today, and all tips, we've got $1,053 this month," Tia said finally. She had a smudge of dirt on her nose and a blueberry stain on her arm.

"No way!" I said. "Even after we pay for the last of the ice, that makes almost two thousand dollars. That's like a thousand dollars each. Incredible!"

We stood up in the barn, the sunlight filtering through the slats in the wall, the musty smell of dirt clinging to everything, and held hands and hopped around, screaming. Mr. Ramos came running into the barn. When he saw we were happy, he mopped his face and asked, "What is going on here?"

Tia told him and he broke into a big smile. "Of course. Two smart girls. Two good farmers who grew the berries. What else could there be?"

Tia asked him something in Spanish. I saw her dad argue with her a little but couldn't understand. Finally he hugged her and nodded and went back to work.

"What was that about—or is it too nosy to ask?"

"I asked him if he would take me over to Daniel's to give him the money. My dad thought I should save some for myself. But why? My parents are with me, and even if I go back to Mexico, my mother will come with me. And I'm not sick. I'll come back next summer and we can make more and then there will be money for me. Right?"

I nodded. "So are you going back to Mexico, then?"

She looked at me. "Your dad is home. My dad will have to start looking for another job at the end of the season."

My dad hadn't returned from Fort Lewis yet, so I didn't know what to tell her. No decision had been made as far as I knew, but maybe there was something I didn't know. I'd have to ask my dad. Till then, I'd say nothing about that.

"I'm going to wash up and go to Daniel's," Tia said. "Will you pray that he accepts it?"

"Let's pray together right here," I said. We'd never prayed together.

"Okay," she nodded. "Out loud?"

I nodded. We held hands in the middle of the barn. "Dear God, thank you for this money. Please let Daniel take the money with a glad heart. Please let there be a flight that his mom can get on and come right away. Please bless Tia for being so kind in this.

Bring her what she needs in the way only you can do."

Tia whispered, "Thank you, Jesus, for the money, for the berries, for my homes, and for my friends. In your name I pray, amen."

I squeezed her hand. "Go clean up and give him the dough! And let me know first thing in the morning how it goes. I'll meet you at the bridge when we're heading to cheer the team on."

I got home and did the victory dance again with Grammy—except that it was more like a victory polka or waltz with her.

"I'm so proud of you." She hugged me, and her soft arms snuggled me the way they had since I was a small girl. Then I took my dusty self into the shower.

When I got out, Grammy was waiting in my room. "I have an opportunity for you tonight," she said.

"Great!"

"They just called from the church to see if you'd help out in the nursery. The VBS kids are going to have their little performance, and if the moms can leave the little kids in the nursery, they can enjoy it so much more."

"Oh no," I said. "Not kids."

Grammy didn't move.

All of a sudden I remembered my promise—only to myself, of course—at the Before the Bridge party.

If I could help out the VBS teacher, who had been so nice to Tia, then I would.

I sighed. *F* for *faithfulness* was written on my dirty, worn-out shoes. "Okay. Only this once. And if they all end up crying, I take no responsibility."

Papa drove me to the church. No tie this time.

I went to the bathroom as soon as I got there and put a wet paper towel on my forehead. I felt like throwing up. But I didn't.

I stopped in the sanctuary for a minute and sat in a back pew. I came early so I'd be ready when the kids were dropped off. I closed my eyes. *God, please help me do this. Be with me. Don't let me panic. Don't let me be alone.*

In my mind came back a few pieces of the song I'd first heard here at the beginning of the summer, knowing God was talking to me.

Softly and tenderly Jesus is calling,
Calling for you and for me;
See, on the portals He's waiting and watching,
Watching for you and for me.

Watch for me. Wait for me. Meet me there and everywhere, Jesus. I need you.

By the time they were all checked in, there were only three little kids in the toddler nursery. "I'll be right across the way with the infants if you need me," Mrs. Jenkins, the mail lady, said. "Just shout."

I hoped I didn't have to shout. At first the kids all stood in the corner. The room had a bookshelf with board books and a box of blocks in the corner. A little pretend kitchen was off to the side. One of the kids started crying, and the other two must have thought it was a good idea because they started in, too. Mrs. Jenkins was trying not to be obvious about peeking over the half door separating the rooms, but I saw her. I also saw a box of teddy bear-shaped graham crackers on the counter.

"Cookies!" I said. Licorice worked for Pablo. Why not cookies? I got the box and sat on the floor and shook the box.

One little boy stopped crying. "Gookie?" he asked.

"Yes, gookies for the next hour!" I promised. "As long as you're quiet." I hoped the parents wouldn't mind.

The other two came over, too, their diapers making soft cushy sounds like air rushing out of balloons as they plopped on the floor. "Gookie?"

Once I got cookies into all of them, I grabbed the books from the shelf. "How about this one? *Make Way for Ducklings*?"

I read it out loud and quacked. The little boy in the soccer shorts laughed. He thought I was funny! It was addicting! I quacked again and again till they were all laughing.

We played kitchen for a while, too, till I was tired

of eating pretend plastic egg after pretend plastic egg.

"Let's get more cookies," I suggested.

"Gookies!" Everyone shouted with glee. We all four sat on the floor. The little girl brought me a book. It was *Pat the Bunny*. My eyes teared up. Gary had just bought that for the baby. Our baby.

By the time all of the parents came and got their kids, I was worn out.

"How'd it go?" Papa asked on the way home.

"Okay. For once. I mean, anyone can do it once, right?" I asked.

Papa winked. He knew, deep inside, how much that had meant to me. Those kids liked me. Not just the cookies. Me.

⌇

We all drove over to the bridge and lined up our cars the next day. There must have been like twenty cars. It was so cool. Tia came in my car, because her dad was working. She said her cousin Sara was going to meet us by the freeway, on the way to the coast, and Daniel was, too.

"So how did it go with Daniel?" I asked.

"He took it," she said, beaming. "He wasn't going to at first, but Orlando was there and he convinced him. I've never really seen a guy cry before. I turned away when he did, to give him some privacy. One of the women at our church is a travel agent, and when they called her, she got right online. They got a ticket with enough left over for his mom to buy some new clothes when she gets here, so she feels good at the hospital, you know, talking with everyone."

"New clothes always make a woman feel good, don't they?" I asked. I'd worn my same old jean shorts and running shoes, but I wore my new board shirt, the pink one that made my tan look great, and tucked my hair back behind one ear. I wanted to look good this morning. I wished it was me on the team, but at least I'd be cheering for Charlie and Natalie.

"Yeah," Tia said, picking at her old shorts. She'd spent what little money she had on the light blue dress for Felicia's Quince.

"Anyway, Daniel said to tell you thanks," Tia said.

"I didn't do anything. Except eat too many smoothies." I patted my tummy. Good thing they were mostly fruit and yogurt.

We pulled up to the Park and Ride lot where everyone was parking their cars. We would stand alongside the road while the Hood to Coast runners came by. I stood with Grammy and Papa and Tia. Her cousin Sara drove up with her family—I recognized some of them from the Quince and the soccer game.

Tia shook a graham cracker at me. "Want one?"

"No, but that reminds me." I told her about the

nursery the night before. "I was brave enough to try since you tried with the money," I told her. "Thanks for the example."

She smiled. We stood by the side of the road and I felt a tap on my shoulder. I turned around.

"*Charlie*!" I gasped. "What are you doing here? You're supposed to be in Portland. What happened? Are you injured?" He should have been several miles into his run, not standing on the sidelines with the rest of us.

"I'm not running. Kiski cut me," he simply said. "And he was right to, because I would have dragged the team down."

"Why?"

"I couldn't make the practices at the end."

I don't know if it was by plan or just wisdom, but everyone around us seemed to give us some space.

"Why not?"

He didn't answer. Suddenly it all came clear. He was at the booth. The practices *hadn't* all been held at night as I had assumed. Charlie had missed them to help out at the Pink Palace after Tia had been hurt.

"It was because of the smoothies, wasn't it?"

He looked down at the ground. "You need new shoes," was all he said.

I put my hand on his shoulder. "Thank you, Charlie. You should know that Tia's friend Daniel, the guy who is having the operation, can have his mom come and stay with him now. Because you stayed at the booth."

"Oh, that's cool. I didn't do it for Daniel, though." He grew pink. I did, too.

Tia was standing back, looking puzzled. I knew she was wondering why Charlie wasn't running. The crowd started whistling, cheering, and blowing air horns. The team was coming! Charlie and I joined the others on the side of the road, jostling for the best view. We all clapped and cheered as they ran by. One by one, as they ran past Charlie, they each took their caps off of their heads and made a little bow. Charlie blushed but smiled. They all knew why he'd dropped out.

On the way home I explained it to Tia. At first she felt bad. Then she didn't. "It's in his character, isn't it?" she asked.

"Yes. He loves to tease, but down deep, he's a tender and great guy. Just like it's in your character to give Daniel your money."

When we got home my dad's car was there. He must know, by now, if he was staying or going. I leaped out of the car the minute Papa shut it off. I ran into the house. "Dad?" I called.

"I'm in here, sugar," he said. "Gary just called. Your mom is having the baby right now."

When I was a little girl, my parents would take me to the Puyallup Fair for my birthday. Some people like to eat the scones the best. They're good, dripping with strawberries and whipped cream. Some people like the loud concerts or the Gentleman Jugglers or the pig races. I like the rides. The ones I like best are the wild rides.

Neither my mom nor my dad likes the wild rides, but I do. I mean, what is the sense of going on a ride if you know exactly how it is going to go? Who wants to get on those little tin boats that go round and round in two feet of water? Not me. I wanted the roller coaster—the one where I couldn't see the dips and rises before we were there. I knew I was safe and that the people who loved me would always buckle me in.

That's kind of what life is like with my mom and my dad. A roller coaster. I knew I was buckled in, but I still felt the pit in my gut because I didn't know what dips and rises lay just ahead.

CHAPTER FIFTEEN

They had decided to induce my mom—give her some medicine that would bring the baby along. The contractions had gone on pretty long, and they were worried that the baby might be getting too weak. The baby! *I* was getting weak, because by early the next morning the baby still hadn't been born. Another three hours and they'd give her a Cesarean—surgery to take the baby out. I talked with Gary and then hung up the phone. I wished I could be there. Not that I could do anything. I didn't mention anything about my choice to Gary, of course, even though I'd made my decision. I needed to talk with my mom, first. And my dad.

"Should we go and do something while we wait?" Dad asked me.

"Yeah," I said. "Let me get my sweat jacket." I ran upstairs. When I got there I dropped to my knees at the side of my bed. *Please let my mom be okay, God. Let the baby be safe. Don't let anyone be sick or injured or whatever. Help Gary be okay, too.*

Gary had been trying to sound smooth for me, but I could tell he was worried.

"How about the farmers' market?" Dad said to me. It was Saturday, so it was open early. There'd be lots of Portlanders there, but Dad enjoyed going, too.

"Sounds good." We drove to the market, a few miles away, in silence. The peaches hung low on the trees as we passed the orchards. Their fragrance blew in through the open windows. If I could bottle any perfume, I'd bottle one that smelled like fresh peaches. If you closed your eyes you could almost feel the fuzz on your lips and the sticky juice trickling down your chin. Hey! Maybe that'd be my next business.

The wind blew through my hair, and I could hear the shouts of kids squeezing the last bits of summer out of the month. We pulled up to the farmers' market. We knew most of the farmers here—small-time farmers who grew vegetables and flowers, not commercial farmers like Papa and Grammy or the Richardses.

Dad bought some peaches—even though we could have picked some from friends for free—and some corn on the cob.

"Do you know what my favorite meal is, Meggie?" he asked.

I bit into a peach and shook my head.

"Fresh tomatoes, sliced thick, with salt sprinkled across them. Supersweet corn on the cob boiled right after it's picked, with butter dripping down it so fast you have to keep rolling the cob as you eat it. And cucumbers with vinegar splashed on them—just enough to pucker your mouth when you take a bite. You can't get that kind of food in the army, I'll tell you. Only right here at home."

I smiled. See? He thought of the Island as his home, too. We'd be very happy here. He'd see.

Several men came up and talked with Dad. Friends from childhood, people he'd known a long time. That kind of friend can be very comfortable, and Dad laughed easily. I noticed, though, that while they had on overalls and work boots, Dad wore pressed jeans and penny loafers. His nails were clean, too.

Dad bought some tomatoes, and I pointed out some Kirby cucumbers—the ones that looked like knobby little roots, not the long skinny ones. We bought two more peaches the size of softballs and drove over to our tree house to eat them.

We left the bags in the car and climbed up the sturdy stairs and sat down. I took off my sweat jacket. The day had already burned off the early morning cool.

"I wish you'd have been here when the peas were out," I said. "We had the good kind—the crinkled, wrinkled kind. I don't like the normal ones. I like the ones that are different."

"You and I are different, that's why," Dad said. "I learned long ago that while there were some things about me that are like the farmers on the Island, there are some things that are not."

"Like what?"

"Like that plaque in your room," Dad said.

Aha! I'd finally get to hear the story. I looked down at my tired old dogs and saw the letter *P*. My patience had paid off.

"I don't know how old I was," Dad said. "But the FFA, Future Farmers of America, sponsored a contest for all of the boys—and some girls—on the Island. We had to come up with some innovative way of growing plants or processing them or even taking care of pests without using as many chemicals. We spent a good year working on our projects. Some of my friends tried developing hybrids, like Papa did with the strawberries. I think that's what Papa had hoped I would try. He was interested in that even then. He wanted us to work on it together."

I took a bite of my peach and licked my lower lip, quick, before the juice escaped. "But you weren't?"

Dad shook his head. "No. I wasn't interested in chemicals, either. Or in ways to harvest berries better."

"But you must have done something," I said. "Or you wouldn't have gotten a plaque."

"I wrote a research paper on how the military had freeze-dried fruit for the troops in the service."

"Oh. Well, that had something to do with fruit."

Dad laughed out loud. "See how smart you are? You realize, too, that's not what they were looking for. But it was what I was looking for. I tried to fit what my dad wanted—farming—in with something I wanted—the military. I did pretty good for a young kid trying to keep a foot in both worlds. You can't really do that, though. Eventually you have to choose one world to live in and one to visit."

"And you chose the military," I said, watching the dust motes float in the river of light streaming through the slats of the tree fort.

"I did. For a while I hid my desires away—like stuffing that plaque where I wouldn't have to look at it. I finally realized I had a choice. So I made it." He reached over and touched my hand. "And now I have another choice—we have a choice. Do I stay on Sau-

vie Island and farm, or do I stay with the military in
Washington, D.C.?"

"When do we have to make the decision?" I
asked. I already had made it, earlier, but now I wasn't
so sure. I needed more time to think.

"Soon," Dad said. "School starts soon, and I have
to let my higher-ups know."

The cell phone rang. Dad saw the number and
handed it to me. "It's your mom."

I greedily snatched the phone. "Hello?"

"Hi, Meg," came the tired voice on the other side.
"I'm fine, and someone else wants to say hello to
you." I heard high-pitched crying in the background.
"It's your brother, Elliot."

My brother. *My* brother. My *brother*. Goose
bumps ran up my arm.

Elliot. What a cool name.

"Are you okay?" I asked my mom.

"Oh yes, I'm fine," Mom said. "They had to do it
by operation, so it'll take me a little bit longer to
recover, but I'm fine and so is the baby. Oh, Meg, I
can't wait for you to meet him. He looks just like
you!"

"Poor kid," I joked, but secretly I was glad. Wrinkled peas of the world, unite!

We chatted for just a few more minutes, and then
my mom hung up to take a nap. She'd been up all
night. She promised to call me in the evening after
she'd rested awhile.

I gave Dad the news and saw a strange look cross his face. He'd told me before that if he'd had it to do over again, he'd do things differently. There was no point in talking about that now.

I looked at my watch. "Tia's family invited us to play soccer with them this afternoon. Want to go?"

"You bet!" We hopped into the car and drove home to change. Dad handed the farmers' market bags over to Grammy for lunch.

"Elliot's here!" I sang out. "And he looks like me."

Papa smiled. "Then he's on his way to a fine life." I hugged Papa. What other grandpa in the world could be so great? I hugged Grammy. What other grandma?

We drove out to the soccer fields. Tia's family and friends were already playing. "Join us!" said Mr. Ramos. This time the Spanish chatter went on as we passed. A few people recognized me from the Quince and stopped to say hello.

I played defense and my dad played attack. We were on the same team, of course. We always would be. Although we didn't understand the Spanish and most of the players didn't speak English, we all understood the game without needing to speak. How cool would it be to play soccer with my dad all the time? He gave me a high five as we walked off the field. Tia stood on the sidelines, still recovering, and clapped.

Later that afternoon, after our vegetarian feast, I

went up to my room to change once again, making sure my clothes got into the hamper. I sat on my bed, took the plaque in both hands, and read the last three verses, John 15:10, 11, and 12.

"If you obey my commands, you will remain in my love, just as I have obeyed my Father's commands and remain in his love. I have told you this so that my joy may be in you and that your joy may be complete. My command is this: Love each other as I have loved you."

How do I do that, Lord?

"Greater love has no one than this, that he lay down his life for his friends," it went on in verse 13.

I snuck out to the fields, making sure no one saw me. In between the rails of spent raspberry canes, I knelt.

I'm sorry I've asked you over and over to do things for me, Lord. I am so glad you're talking to me and I can hear you. I am so glad you're helping me to be fruitful. I am so glad you want to be with me and use me to show your love and fruit with others. Jesus, what should I do?

Then I did something I hardly ever do. I sat still and stayed quiet till I heard back from Him. When I did, in the quietness of my heart, I knew what I needed to do next. I got up from my knees and brushed the dirt off of them. I walked back into the house and put my shorts back on.

"Dad?" He was sitting in the family room watching television. "Can you take me into Portland?"

When I was a baby, I had a soft blankee. It was made out of chenille—you know, that knobby fabric that is sometimes on old people's bedspreads? Anyway, it had silk all around the edges that I used to rub when I sucked my thumb or when I felt nervous. I still have my blankee, tucked away in the very back of my closet at home. Grammy made my blankee for me. I think every kid should have a blankee. Sometimes I wish it was still okay for me to hug it now.

CHAPTER SIXTEEN

First thing on Sunday we went to church. I sat in the backseat of the Caddie with Grammy while Papa drove. My dad wore his uniform. When he got his new rank, he'd have a full eagle on his shoulder patches. "There's nothing as handsome as a man in a uniform," Grammy said proudly. I know that even though she is lonely for dad when he's gone, she's proud of the work he does. Hardly anyone gets to be a full bird colonel.

Papa snapped his best Sunday suspenders. "Like this uniform?" he joked. We all laughed with him. It's good that some things never change when other things always do.

During the church service I slipped my envelope into the little bag that came by to take the tithes and offerings. Inside was one hundred dollars in cash. On the outside of the envelope I had written, "Vacation Bible School—next year." Maybe that would allow them to stock enough cookies for the nursery. I wanted there to be plenty when it was my turn to work again.

I sat all snuggled between the three of them, feeling really good. I saw Charlie on the way out. He looked like "a scrubbed potato," as Grammy would say, all clean and spiffed up. He had new running shoes on. They looked great. "Can I stop over later this afternoon?" I asked him.

"Sure," he said. "Any special reason?"

I nodded. "I'll tell you then."

We drove home and Dad and I sat on the porch while Grammy made lunch. I looked across the property to Tia's house. Her mom had added a few new geranium patches, and Mr. Ramos was out on the property fixing one of the machines. I was sure he'd have it running.

"So you feel pretty set on this?" my dad asked. We'd talked about it last night, of course, in Portland.

"Yep. I think it's the right thing to do."

"For who?" Dad asked. "For Tia? For me? For your mother? Or for you?" The wind blew through my hair, and the rockers creaked *yes, no, stay, go* as we swayed back and forth on them. I could smell the peach fields in the distance and see the cloud of thick dust that Mr. Ramos was stirring up. For one moment my love for the Island hurt. "For all of us," I finally answered. "Like you said yesterday, you can't have a foot in two worlds. You have to belong to one at a time. Just because I won't live here now doesn't mean I never will."

"Same for me," Dad said.

"You belong in the army," I said.

"I do," Dad answered. That was why I was like my dad. Other people might have said, "We can make do wherever," or "I can be wherever I need to be," but Dad told the straight-up. I think, in the long run, that made it easier.

"And I belong with Mom."

"You do," Dad said. "And Gary is good to you, too."

"He's not you," I defended.

"He doesn't have to be," Dad said. "And now you've got a brother."

A brother. I hoped he'd like teddy-shaped graham crackers. And a sister who quacks like a duck when she reads to him.

"I'll buy you a Blackberry and you can text message or email me anytime at all. I'll be in Washington,

D.C., so it won't be that far away. Next Christmas we'll go to Europe with Grammy and Papa."

I smiled. It did sound like fun.

"Lunch!" Grammy hollered through the screen door. We went in and sat in the dining room. She had all of her fine china and silverware out.

"Looks lovely, dear," Papa said. His scalp was really red. Grammy's eyes were, too.

"Let's eat!" I said, and that broke the tension. We laughed and joked, and even Grammy's eyes were bright when we talked about visiting Europe together next Christmas.

"I never thought I'd get there," she said. I knew she'd be thinking of what kind of presents she could bring home for her friends—and the bragging she'd do on her son. After lunch we chatted for a few minutes and then I excused myself.

"I'd better go and say good-bye before Dad and I leave," I said. My dad would be taking me to Seattle in an hour or two. I was eager to get home and help Mom, but not eager to talk with Charlie and Tia. I grabbed my backpack and headed out the door.

Charlie first. As I walked to his house, I casually considered how big the acreage would be if his farm and our farm became one someday.

I knocked on his door. Charlie answered. I could tell by the look on his face that he knew I was saying good-bye.

"You're going back to Seattle, aren't you?" he asked.

I nodded. We sat on the steps. "My mom needs my help. I need to get to know my brother. My dad needs to be in the army—and the Ramoses need to be here."

"Will you be back next summer?" he asked.

"Next summer and every summer," I said. "I hope there's room for me on the Portland to Coast team."

"If you get some new shoes there will be," he joked. "I'll miss you," he finished in a softer voice.

As I headed down the stairway, Charlie called out, "Meg!" I turned around, and as I did he took his cap off and bowed toward me, at my decision, like the Portland to Coast team had for him yesterday. I smiled and waved.

I walked slowly over to Tia's house and knocked. Pablo came to the door. "Licorice?" he asked. I handed him a large unopened bag of his very own. "¡Gracias!" he shouted and ran to his room.

Tia came out. "Hi . . ." she said and looked at me curiously.

"I came to say good-bye," I said.

"Good-bye?" she shouted. "Where are you going?"

"To Seattle." I explained about Elliot, and her eyes shone with tears of sorrow and of joy for me.

"You will make the best big sister. Look at Pablo! He'd probably like to stow away in your car and go with you rather than stay here with me!" she said. Her face grew serious then. "Is this the right thing to do?"

"Yes," I said. I remembered the verse on the plaque. Love asked me to lay down my life for others. For my dad. For my friend. For my mother. And in return, God would give me the life I could never give myself.

"It's in your character," Tia said softly. "You'll be back next summer? If you come back, I can tell you how to make gobs of money."

We both laughed hard and hugged. I gave her my address. "Write to me, and I'll write to you. We'll make plans for next summer. Okay?"

She nodded. "I could never have asked for a better friend than you. You'll be a dama at my Quince, right?"

"Wouldn't miss it," I said. I handed a card to her. "Please don't open that till later. Maybe tomorrow, okay?"

She nodded. "Okay. Wait here." She ran out to the property between her house and mine and picked a handful of wild flowers. Then she got a knit string and tied them together. "Dry them when you get home. For memories."

I promised I would. The summer ended as it had begun, with a posy of flowers from an unexpected friend. We were not "old" and "new" girls anymore, and her parents and Grammy and Papa weren't old and new Islanders anymore, I think. We were "us." Together.

At Grammy's I packed the blue blanket I had knit for Elliot—not knowing I had been knitting it for him, of course. "Can I take this devotional?" I called to Grammy.

"Of course. I'll have another one next summer!" she hollered back. I heard the pleasure in her voice. It would be the first devotional I'd ever taken back with me.

"Take care of Tia for me," I told Grammy. She smiled. At first I didn't want to share Grammy with Tia. I knew my place was my place, though, with Dad, with Grammy and Papa, with my mom and Gary. With Elliot! I didn't need to clasp so tightly anymore to something I would never lose.

My dad was anxious to get going. I know he wasn't really looking forward to seeing my mom and Gary and the baby, even though he liked them all. It was awkward. Nobody likes to drive over the bumps in the road, but we all have to do it.

I wondered what kind of clothes Tia would buy with the Nordstrom Rack gift card I'd bought in Portland with Dad, the one I'd slipped into her card. All of my smoothie money—minus the donation to the VBS program—would go a long way toward buying her clothes for school. I had planned to give her enough for a new jean skirt. But now she could buy pretty much whatever else she wanted. Not in baby blue, I hoped. It wasn't her best color.

A month after I returned home, I got a letter in the mail. I held Elliot in one arm, cradling his head in the crook of my elbow while I opened the letter. A check fluttered out. Wow! It was made out to me. I picked up the check and grinned. It would buy a lot of new running shoes. I read:

Dear Meg,

You'll be so proud to know that the university has patented Papa's hybrid strawberries. He named the berry breed "Nutmeg" after his favorite strawberry blonde. It seemed only fair—you spent summer after summer working in the fields with Papa. Consider this part of your payment—a couple of years late. The new plant, and the girl it's named after, is sweet, strong, and bears much fruit. The patent is in your name and ours, so the royalty checks will come to us from now on, but spend this one on yourself. We'll put the others aside for your college fund and to keep up the farm. After all, the farm will be yours one day.

Kiss that baby for me. We love you.

Grammy and Papa

*If your first concern is to look after yourself,
you'll never find yourself. But if you forget
about yourself and look to me, you'll find both
yourself and me.*

Matthew 10:39 THE MESSAGE

Connect with other FRIENDS FOR A SEASON readers at *www.FriendsforaSeason.com!*

- Sign up for Sandra Byrd's newsletter
- Send e-cards to your friends
- Download FRIENDS FOR A SEASON wallpapers and icons
- Get a sneak peek at upcoming books in the series
- Learn more about the places and events featured in each book

www.FriendsforaSeason.com